The Scarlet Rose

"I Knew I'd Meet You"

STORY & ART BY

PATRICIA LYFOUNG

COLOR BY

PHILIPPE OGAKI

NEW YORK

To my little prince and his faithful steed.

By Patricia Lyfoung
La Rose écarlate, volumes 1 and 2, Lyfoung © Éditions Delcourt – 2005/2006
Originally published in French as "Je savais que je te rencontrerais" and
"Je veux que tu m'aimes!"

THE SCARLET ROSE #1
"I Knew I'd Meet You"

Story, art, and cover by Patricia Lyfoung
Color by Philippe Ogaki
Translation by Joe Johnson
Lettering by Bryan Senka

Mariah McCourt – Editor
Jeff Whitman – Assistant Managing Edtior
Jim Salicrup
Editor-in-Chief

PB ISBN: 978-1-62991-826-6
HC ISBN: 978-1-62991-827-3

Charmz is an imprint of Papercutz.

Chamz books may be purchased for business or promotional use.
For information on bulk purchases please contact Macmillan
Corporate and Premium Sales Department at
(800) 221-7945 x5442

Printed in Korea
September 2017

Distributed by Macmillan
First Charmz Printing

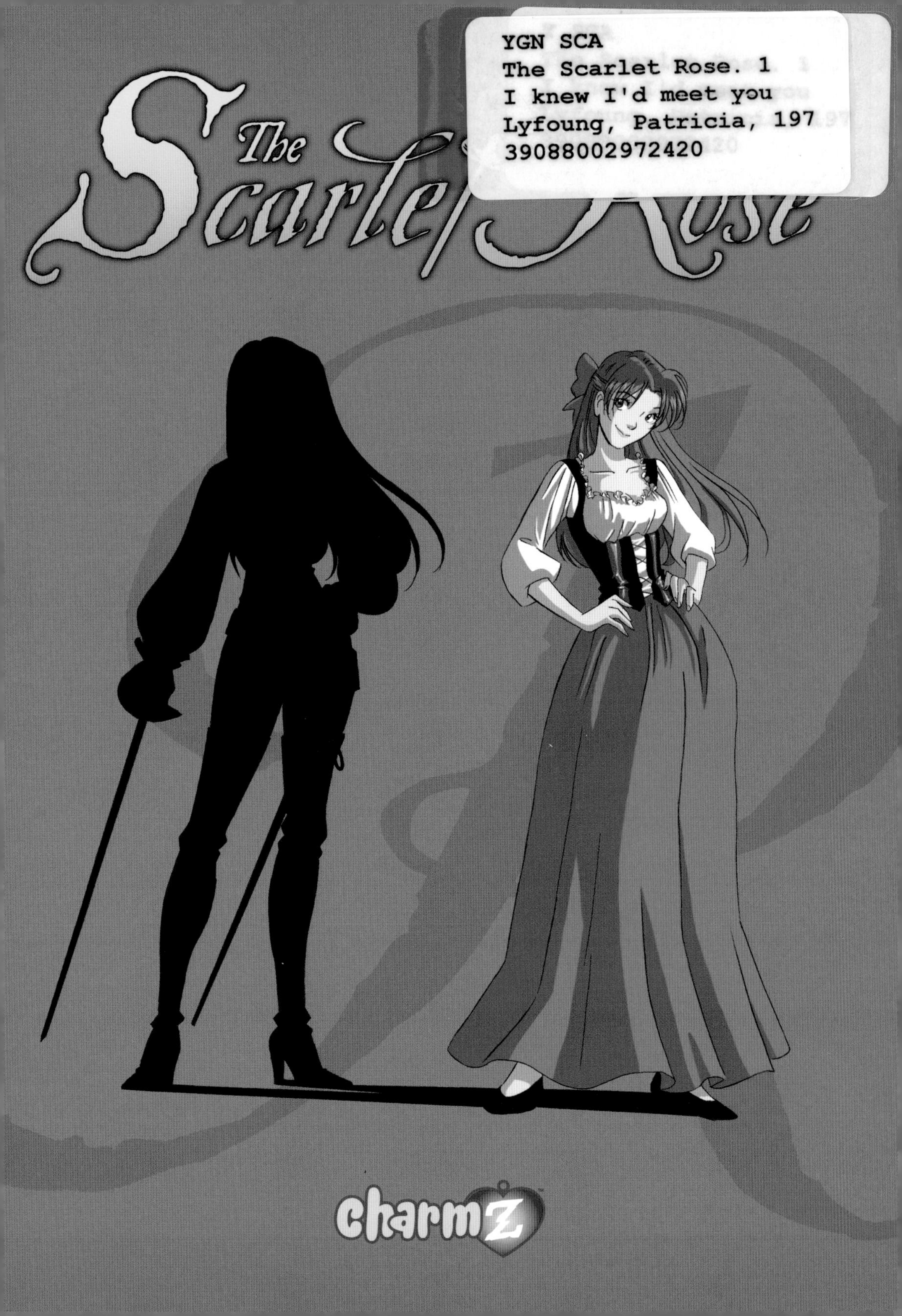
The Scarlet Rose
charmz

MORE GRAPHIC NOVELS AVAILABLE FROM charmZ™

**SWEETIES #1
"Cherry Skye"**

**CHLOE #1
"The New Girl"**

**STITCHED #1
"The First Day of the
Rest of her Life"**

ANA and the COSMIC RACE #1

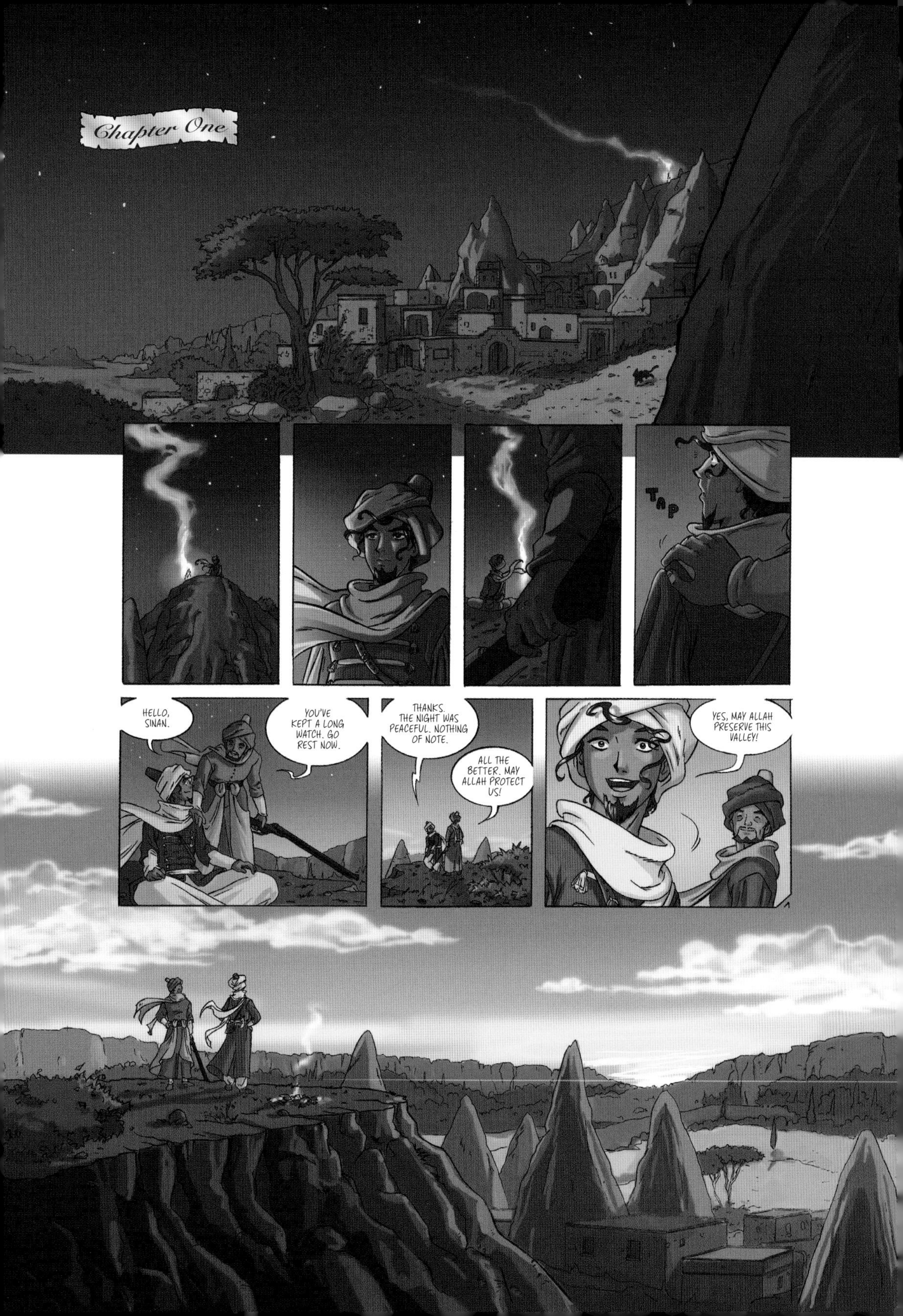
Chapter One
TAP
HELLO, SINAN.
YOU'VE KEPT A LONG WATCH. GO REST NOW.
THANKS. THE NIGHT WAS PEACEFUL. NOTHING OF NOTE.
ALL THE BETTER. MAY ALLAH PROTECT US!
YES, MAY ALLAH PRESERVE THIS VALLEY!

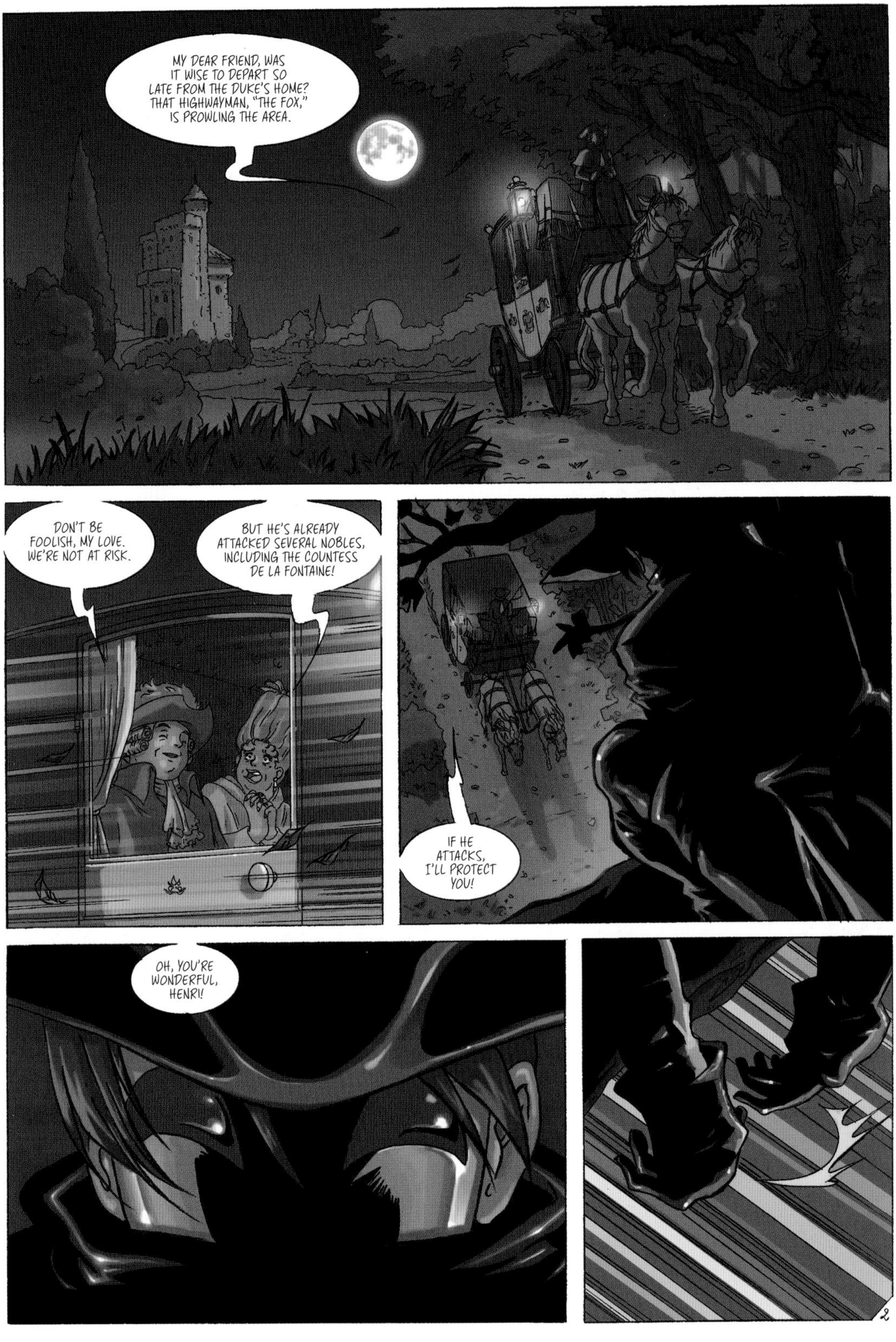
MY DEAR FRIEND, WAS IT WISE TO DEPART SO LATE FROM THE DUKE'S HOME? THAT HIGHWAYMAN, "THE FOX," IS PROWLING THE AREA.
DON'T BE FOOLISH, MY LOVE. WE'RE NOT AT RISK.
BUT HE'S ALREADY ATTACKED SEVERAL NOBLES, INCLUDING THE COUNTESS DE LA FONTAINE!
IF HE ATTACKS, I'LL PROTECT YOU!
OH, YOU'RE WONDERFUL, HENRI!
2

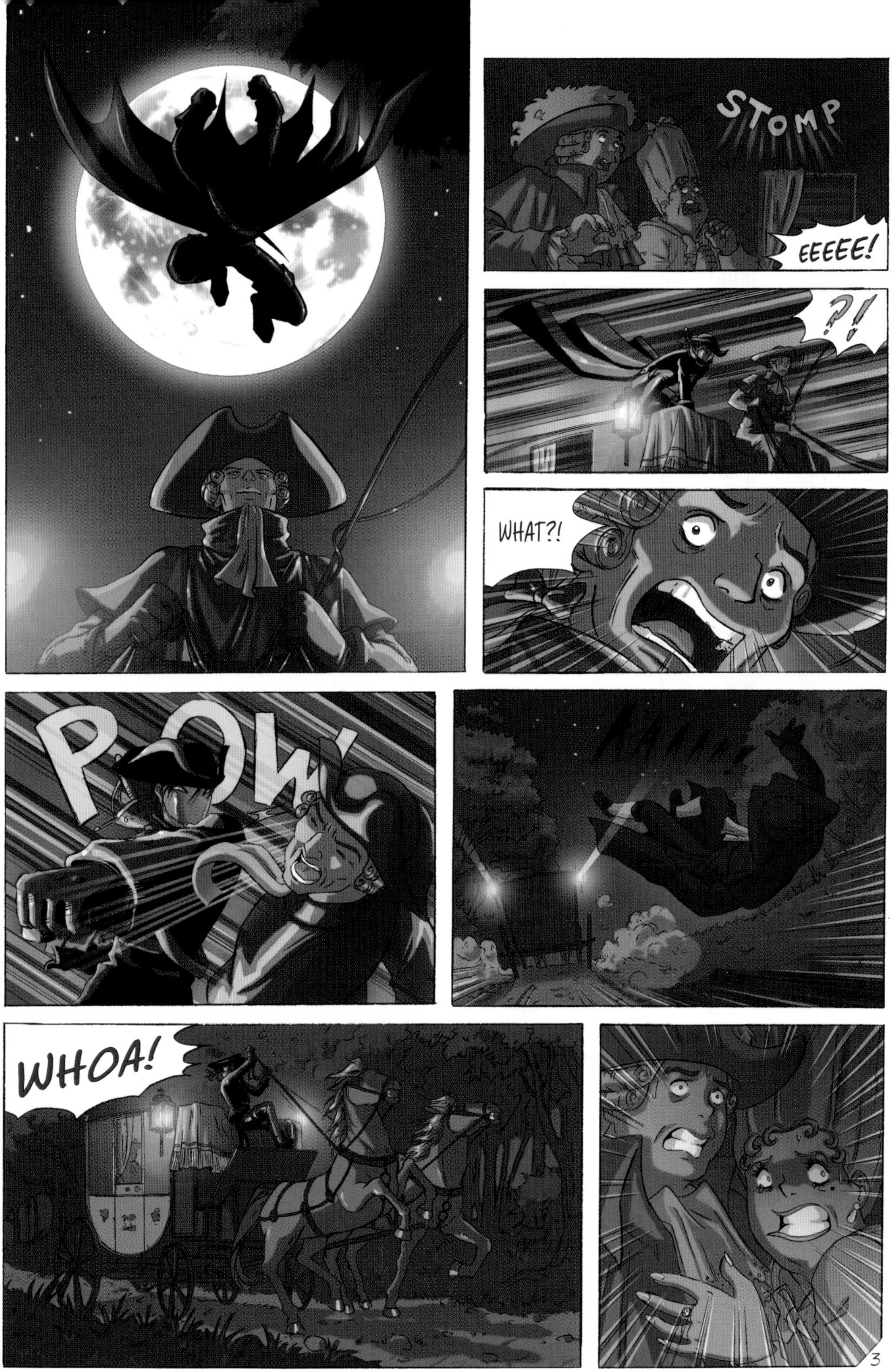
STOMP
EEEEE!
?!
WHAT?!
POW!
WHOA!
3

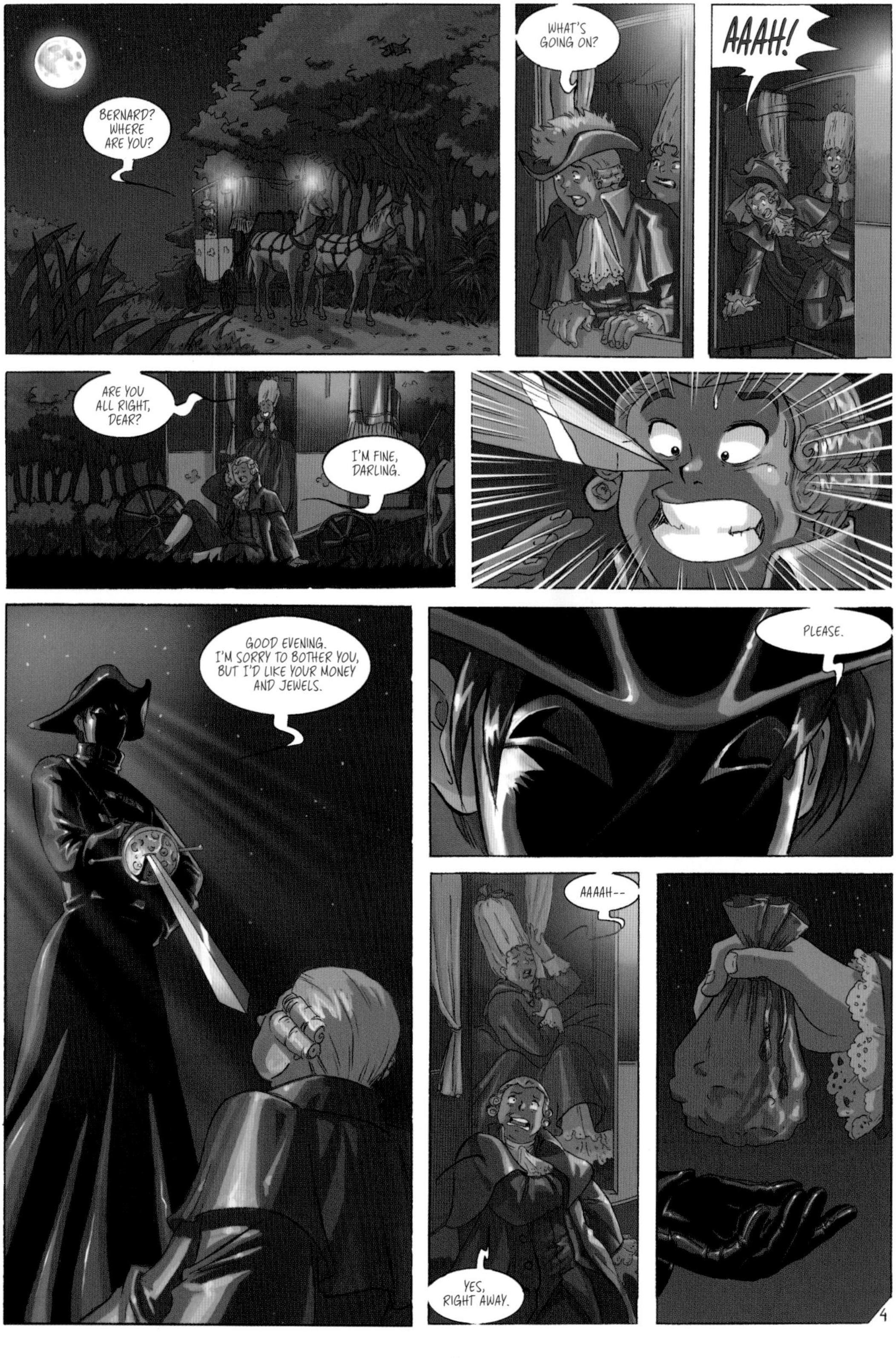
BERNARD? WHERE ARE YOU?
WHAT'S GOING ON?
AAAH!
ARE YOU ALL RIGHT, DEAR?
I'M FINE, DARLING.
GOOD EVENING. I'M SORRY TO BOTHER YOU, BUT I'D LIKE YOUR MONEY AND JEWELS.
PLEASE.
AAAAH--
YES, RIGHT AWAY.
4

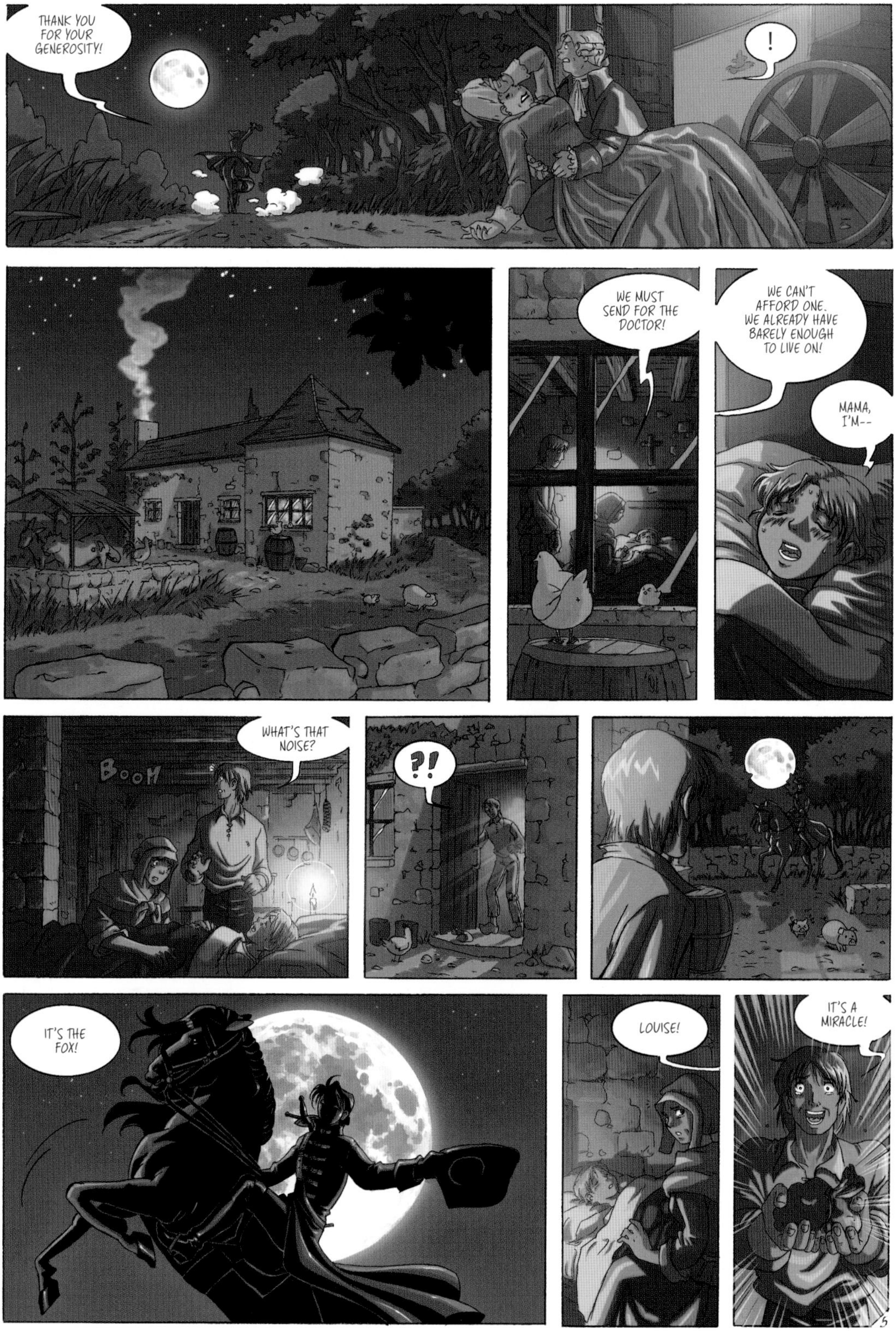
THANK YOU FOR YOUR GENEROSITY!
!
WE MUST SEND FOR THE DOCTOR!
WE CAN'T AFFORD ONE. WE ALREADY HAVE BARELY ENOUGH TO LIVE ON!
MAMA, I'M--
BOOM
WHAT'S THAT NOISE?
?!
IT'S THE FOX!
LOUISE!
IT'S A MIRACLE!
5

...AND WHOEVER CAPTURES THE BANDIT KNOWN AS THE FOX...

...WILL RECEIVE THE SUM OF 500 CROWNS!

NOBODY WANTS TO CAPTURE THE FOX!

WHAT?!

JUSTICE!

AT LEAST HE GIVES THE MONEY HE STEALS TO PEASANTS!

MAUD, YOU'RE CRAZY!

GUARDS!

CAPTURE THAT GIRL FOR ME!

LET US THROUGH!

QUICK! LET'S RUN!

WHAT ARE YOU DOING?

STOP!

MOVE ASIDE! AHHH!

MAUD, I HATE YOU!

I KNOW!

6

HELLO, MR. LACOTE.

HELLO! YOU LOOK HURRIED, MAUD.

WHAT FOOLISHNESS HAVE YOU DONE NOW?

OH, NOTHING SERIOUS, MR. LACOTE.

BY THE WAY, I'LL RETURN YOUR BOOKS TOMORROW, I PROMISE.

AH, YOUTH.

THEY'RE TALKING ABOUT THE FOX EVEN DOWN HERE IN PERIGORD, WHILE HE'S TARGETING PARIS! IT'S WONDERFUL!

AND I ADORE BEING CHASED LIKE A PIG!

FRANCINE, COME ON, THE FOX IS EXTRAORDINARY!

STEALING FROM THE NOBLES AND GIVING THE MONEY TO THE POOR! WHAT GENEROSITY!

I KNOW YOU ADMIRE THAT MAN, BUT YOU SHOULDN'T DRAW ATTENTION TO YOURSELF LIKE THIS...

7

WHO DREW THE SOLDIERS' ATTENTION?

ME!

MAUD...

I DIDN'T TEACH YOU TO READ AND WRITE SO YOU WOULD DISTURB PUBLIC ORDER.

AH, IT'S DONE. YOU FINISHED IT, PAPA!

DON'T CHANGE THE SUBJECT, PLEASE.

I PROMISE I WON'T DO IT AGAIN. CAN I TOUCH IT?

YES! PIERRE AND I WORKED VERY HARD TO FINISH IT.

BUT YOU DID PRACTICALLY EVERYTHING, MR. JEAN-BAPTISTE!

LOOK, FRANCINE, THIS SWORD IS MAGNIFICENT! I'M BESIDE MYSELF!

ME, TOO.

OH, WOW!

OH! IT'S SO BEAUTIFUL!

8

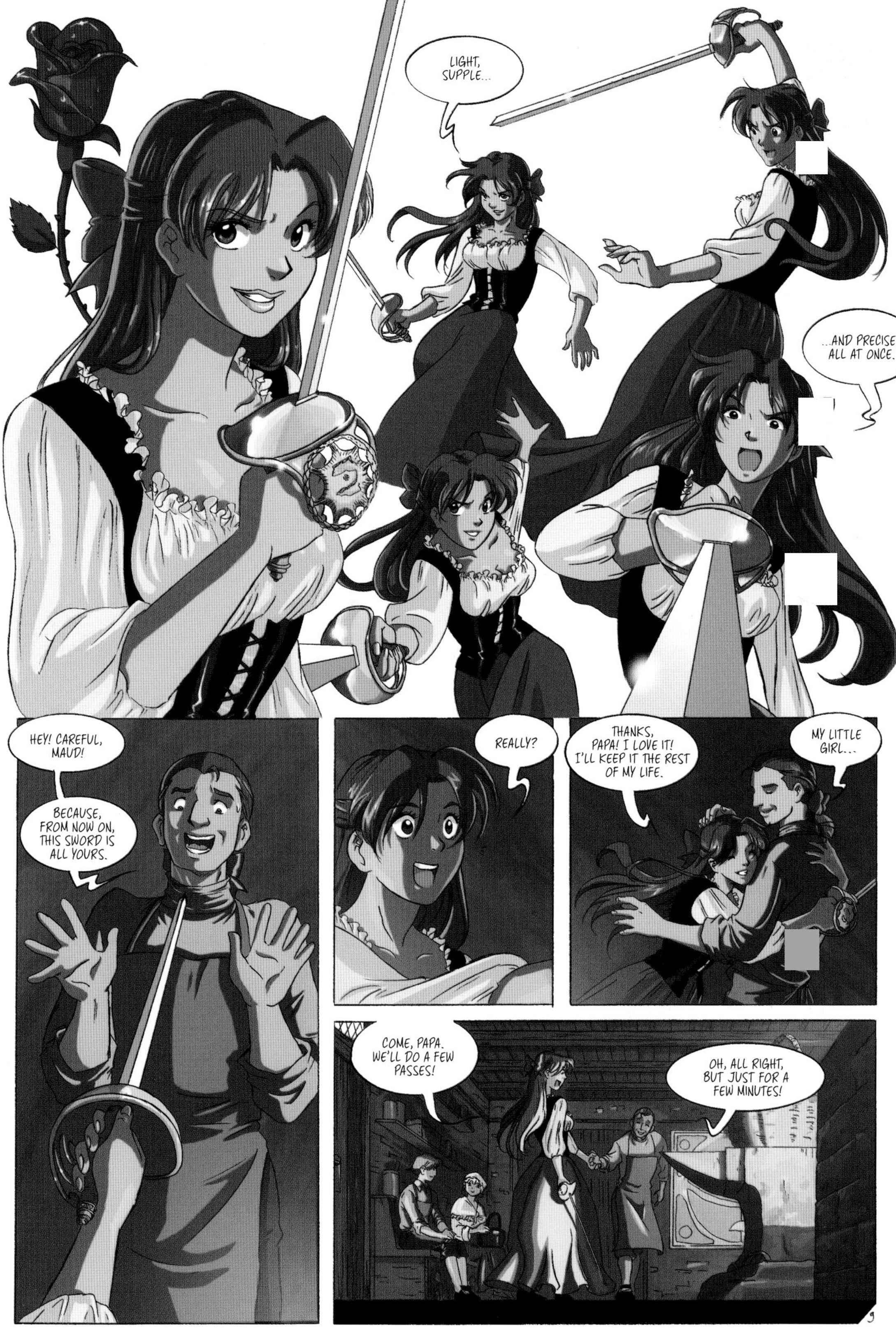
LIGHT, SUPPLE...
...AND PRECISE, ALL AT ONCE.
HEY! CAREFUL, MAUD!
BECAUSE, FROM NOW ON, THIS SWORD IS ALL YOURS.
REALLY?
THANKS, PAPA! I LOVE IT! I'LL KEEP IT THE REST OF MY LIFE.
MY LITTLE GIRL...
COME, PAPA. WE'LL DO A FEW PASSES!
OH, ALL RIGHT, BUT JUST FOR A FEW MINUTES!

TCHIC
TCHAC

TCHIC
TCHAC
TCHIC

YES! I WIN AGAIN!

SO, DO YOU WANT YOUR REVENGE?

ALL RIGHT, THAT'S ENOUGH. I THINK YOU'VE PROVEN THE STUDENT HAS SURPASSED THE TEACHER.

AND I THINK IT'S TIME FOR DINNER. OUR LITTLE FRANCINE IS ABOUT TO FALL ASLEEP.

YES, SHE MUSTN'T BE LATE GETTING HOME.

OH!

I'LL FIX YOU SOMETHING TO EAT.

WAIT, MAUD!

I CAN DO IT, IF YOU LIKE.

YES, GO DO THE LAUNDRY INSTEAD!

I'LL MAKE YOU A DOUBLE HELPING, THEN. WILL YOU HELP ME, FRANCINE?

YES, COMING!

...

10

WELL, WHAT AN EVENING!

AND PIERRE WAS SAYING I WAS A BAD COOK!

WELL, FRANCINE HELPED ME A LITTLE, BUT HE ATE EVERYTHING!

POOF

→OOF!←
I'M EXHAUSTED!!

THIS SWORD IS WONDERFUL! PAPA SPENT SO MUCH TIME ON IT!

I'LL FINALLY BE ABLE TO IMPROVE MY STYLE AND BECOME THE BEST SWORDSWOMAN IN THE WORLD!

BOOM

WHAT WAS THAT NOISE?

PAPA? WHAT'S GOING ON?

AAAH!

?!

11

15

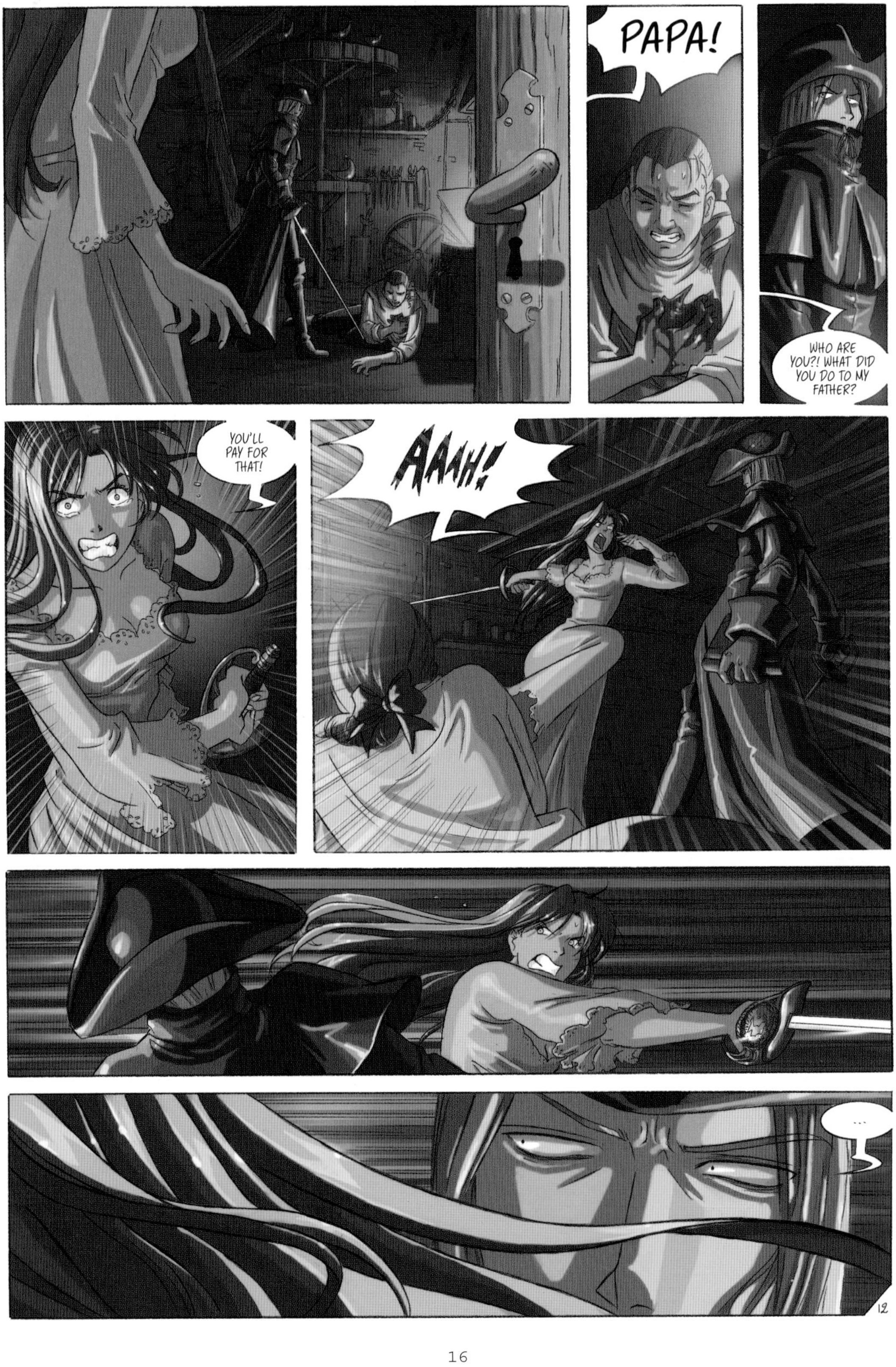
PAPA!
WHO ARE YOU?! WHAT DID YOU DO TO MY FATHER?
YOU'LL PAY FOR THAT!
AAAH!
...
12

AAAAAH!

CLING

VOOSH

AAAH!

FWUMP

!?

LEAVE IT!

AAAH!

13

YOU WRETCH!

BE SEEING YOU!

?!

KRESH

MAUD, NO--

PAPA!

PAPA! YOU'LL BE ALL RIGHT! YOU'LL MAKE IT!

MAUD, KEEP THAT BOOK SAFE. DON'T LET ANYONE TAKE IT.

DON'T TALK. I'LL GO GET THE DOCTOR.

YOU FOUGHT VERY WELL, MY LITTLE GIRL...

14

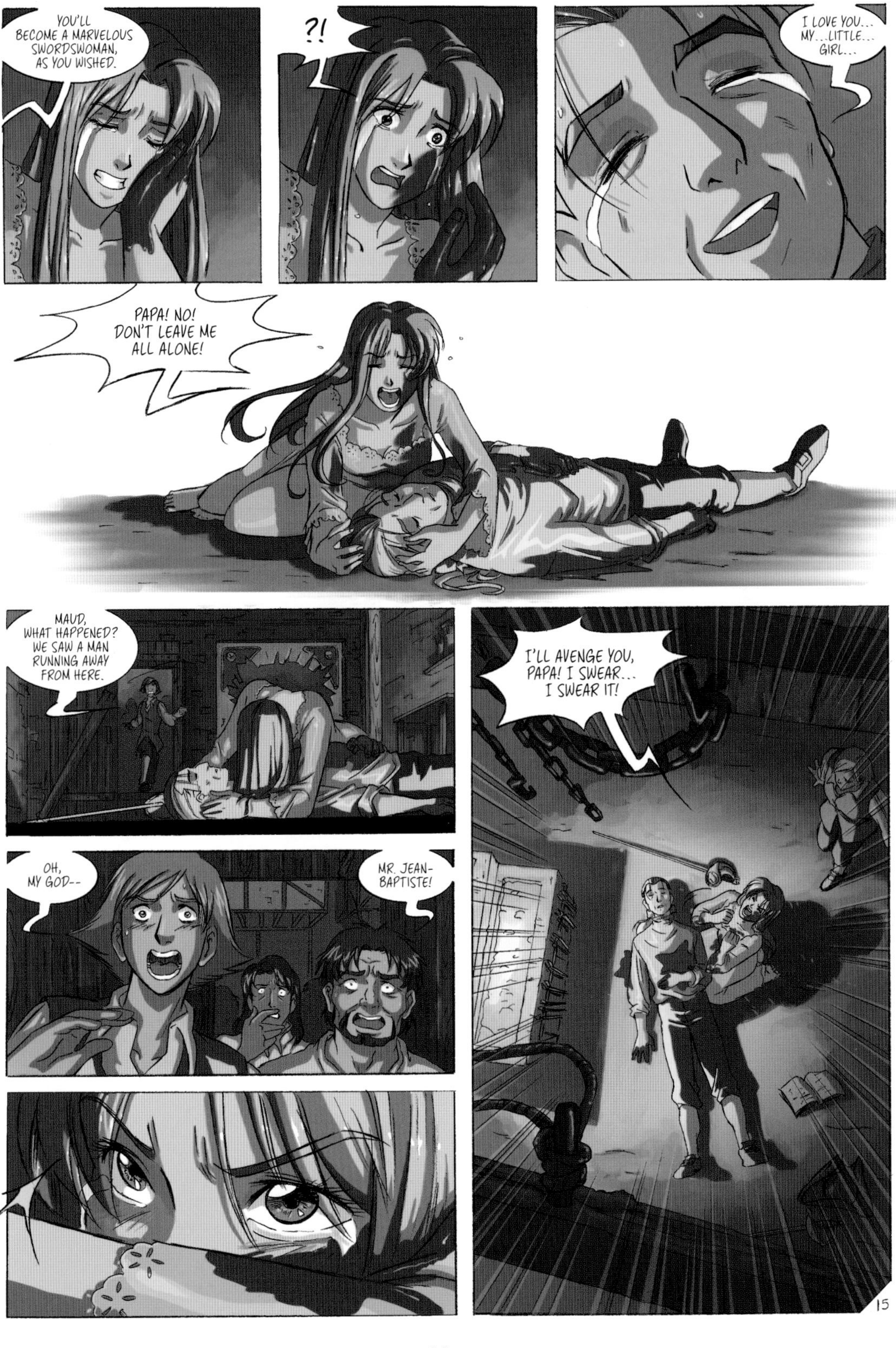
YOU'LL BECOME A MARVELOUS SWORDSWOMAN, AS YOU WISHED.
?!
I LOVE YOU... MY...LITTLE... GIRL...
PAPA! NO! DON'T LEAVE ME ALL ALONE!
MAUD, WHAT HAPPENED? WE SAW A MAN RUNNING AWAY FROM HERE.
OH, MY GOD--
MR. JEAN-BAPTISTE!
I'LL AVENGE YOU, PAPA! I SWEAR... I SWEAR IT!
15

FAREWELL, PAPA. YOU'VE JOINED MAMA IN PARADISE, AND I'M SURE YOU'RE HAPPY.

THE INNKEEPER TOLD ME THE ASSASSIN WAS FROM PARIS. HE ARRIVED THE NIGHT BEFORE AND WAS LOOKING FOR YOUR FATHER'S SMITHY.

HE'S DISAPPEARED. WHAT WILL YOU DO, MAUD?

LEAVE ME ALONE, PLEASE.

MY LITTLE MAUD, PLEASE ACCEPT MY CONDOLENCES.

COME, FRANCINE.

THANKS VERY MUCH, MR. LACOTE.

YOU KNOW, I'M NOT JUST A SIMPLE BOOKSELLER. I'M THE FRIEND OF YOUR GRANDFATHER, THE COUNT DE LAROCHE.

I'M SORRY, THERE'S A MISTAKE. MY GRANDPARENTS ARE ALL DEAD.

NO.

YOUR FATHER, JEAN-BAPTISTE ROCHE HAS ALWAYS HIDDEN YOUR GRANDFATHER'S EXISTENCE FROM YOU.

!?

16

20

BUT WHY?

YOUR GRANDFATHER DIDN'T ACCEPT YOUR FATHER'S MARRIAGE WITH A FOREIGNER AND BANISHED HIM.

HE CAME TO LIVE THE PEACEFUL LIFE OF A SMITH HERE UNTIL HIS TRAGIC END.

THE COUNT AND YOUR FATHER QUARRELED LONG BEFORE YOUR BIRTH.

BUT HOW DO YOU KNOW THIS?

YOUR GRANDFATHER ENTRUSTED ME WITH THE TASK OF LOOKING AFTER YOU, IF SOME MISHAP WERE TO BEFALL YOUR FATHER. TO BRING YOU BACK TO HIM IN PARIS.

MY GRANDFATHER IS A COUNT? A NOBLEMAN? THAT'S IMPOSSIBLE!

YET IT'S TRUE. TELL ME IF YOU DECIDE TO MEET HIM. I'LL AWAIT YOU AT THE BOOKSTORE.

YOUR FATHER'S MURDERER WAS FROM PARIS.

WAIT!

I WANT TO GO TO PARIS!

17

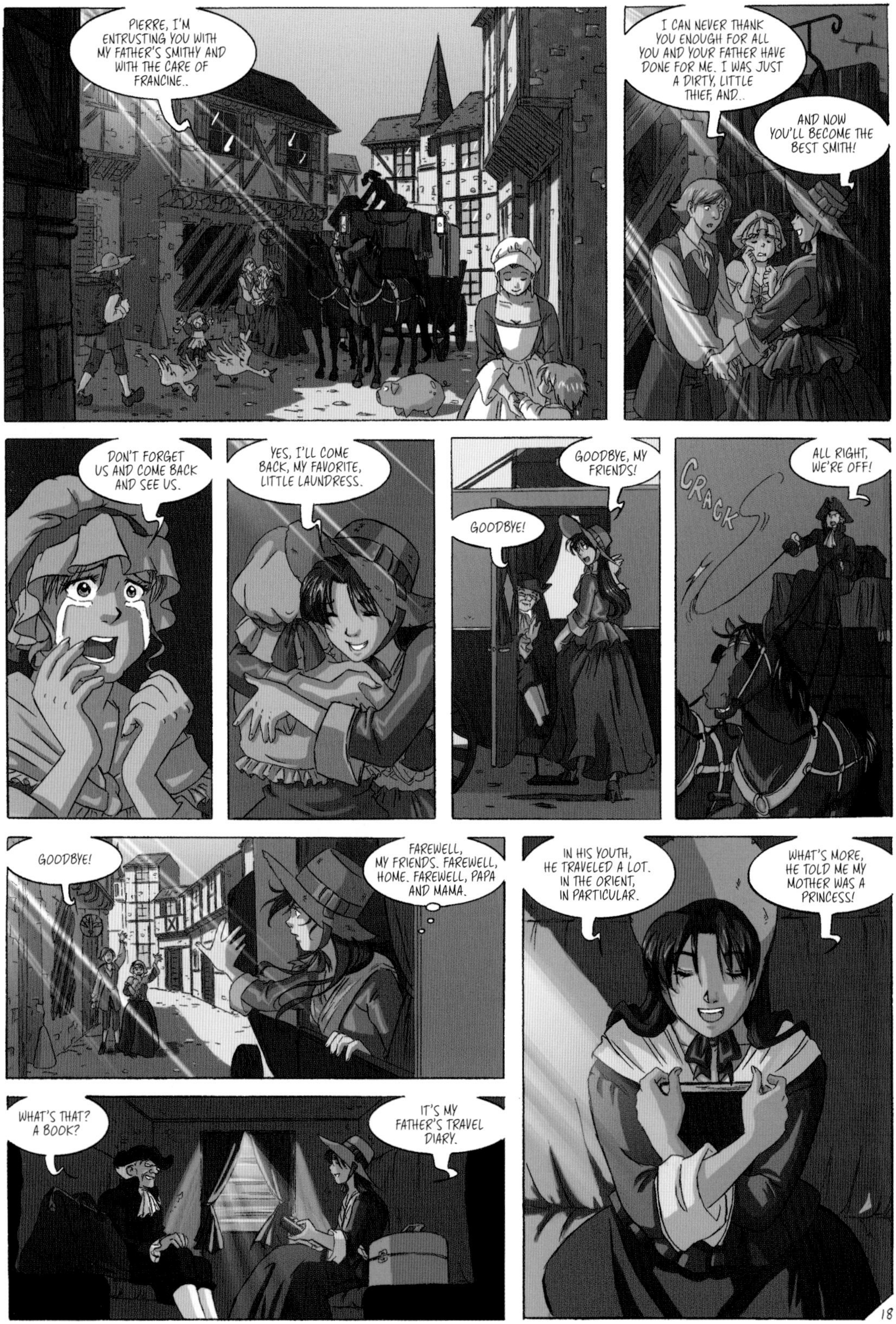
PIERRE, I'M ENTRUSTING YOU WITH MY FATHER'S SMITHY AND WITH THE CARE OF FRANCINE..
I CAN NEVER THANK YOU ENOUGH FOR ALL YOU AND YOUR FATHER HAVE DONE FOR ME. I WAS JUST A DIRTY, LITTLE THIEF, AND..
AND NOW YOU'LL BECOME THE BEST SMITH!
DON'T FORGET US AND COME BACK AND SEE US.
YES, I'LL COME BACK, MY FAVORITE, LITTLE LAUNDRESS.
GOODBYE, MY FRIENDS!
GOODBYE!
CRACKS
ALL RIGHT, WE'RE OFF!
GOODBYE!
FAREWELL, MY FRIENDS. FAREWELL, HOME. FAREWELL, PAPA AND MAMA.
WHAT'S THAT? A BOOK?
IT'S MY FATHER'S TRAVEL DIARY.
IN HIS YOUTH, HE TRAVELED A LOT. IN THE ORIENT, IN PARTICULAR.
WHAT'S MORE, HE TOLD ME MY MOTHER WAS A PRINCESS!
18

AND WAS THAT SO?

I DON'T KNOW!

YES, IT WAS I SUPPOSE. UNFORTUNATELY, FEVER TOOK HER LIFE WHEN I WAS 10. I ESPECIALLY REMEMBER THE SWEETNESS OF HER FACE.

AND MY GRANDFATHER? WHAT'S HE LIKE?

UHM, YOU'LL FIND OUT SOON ENOUGH.

AND AFTER A LONG, EXHAUSTING, TEN-DAY JOURNEY...

WE'VE ARRIVED, MAUD!

WOW.

19

IT'S MAGNIFICENT!

HELLO, EVERYONE!

HELLO! HELLO! HELLO...

WELCOME, MR. LACOTE!

WELCOME, MAM'SELLE MAUD!

I'LL TAKE YOUR THINGS, MR. LACOTE. THE MASTER'S AWAITING YOU IN THE LITTLE SITTING ROOM.

THANKS, PAUL.

MR. LACOTE AND MADEMOISELLE MAUD HAVE ARRIVED, MILORD.

GOOD. LEAVE US, PAUL.

HELLO, CHARLES!

20

HELLO, MY FRIEND!

I'M HAPPY TO SEE YOU AGAIN.

ME TOO. THE CIRCUMSTANCES ARE VERY SAD, BUT HERE WE ARE.

THIS IS YOUR GRANDDAUGHTER. MAUD.

HELLO.

HM.

HOW OLD ARE YOU?

EIGHTEEN, WHY?

YOU'RE OF MARRIAGEABLE AGE.

SORRY?

BUT I DON'T WANT TO GET MARRIED!

YOU'RE IN NO POSITION TO OBJECT!

21

KNOW THAT, FROM NOW ON, YOU'RE UNDER MY ROOF. I'LL MAKE YOU A LADY, MARRY YOU TO A GOOD MATCH, CONTRARY TO WHAT YOUR FATHER DID!

?!

PAUL, TAKE MADEMOISELLE TO HER ROOM.

TOMORROW, SEVERAL TEACHERS WILL TAKE CHARGE OF YOUR EDUCATION.

HAVE YOU GONE MAD, CHARLES?

BUT I DON'T WANT HER TO END UP LIKE HIM!

SHE'LL RECEIVE AN EDUCATION AND WILL HAVE THE RANK SHE DESERVES!

STOP!

THAT CHILD HAS JUST LOST HER FATHER AND SHE'S EXHAUSTED BY THE LONG TRIP!

I KNOW.

SHE RESEMBLES MY SON SO MUCH. IT WAS LIKE SEEING HIM AGAIN.

22

YOU MUST BE TIRED AFTER SUCH A TRIP.

HOW ABOUT A NICE BATH, MADEMOISELLE?

CALL ME MAUD. WE'RE THE SAME AGE, JULIE!

I'D NEVER DARE! YOU'RE A YOUNG LADY, AND I'M A CHAMBERMAID.

VERY WELL, BUT LET'S BE FRIENDS! OTHERWISE I'LL HATE LIVING IN THIS HOUSE.

YET, THE MASTER IS VERY KIND HERE.

I FEEL LIKE HE HATES ME. HE WANTS TO MARRY ME OFF! GO FIGURE!

BUT MY HEART IS ALREADY TAKEN...

REALLY? WHO'S THE LUCKY FELLOW?

23

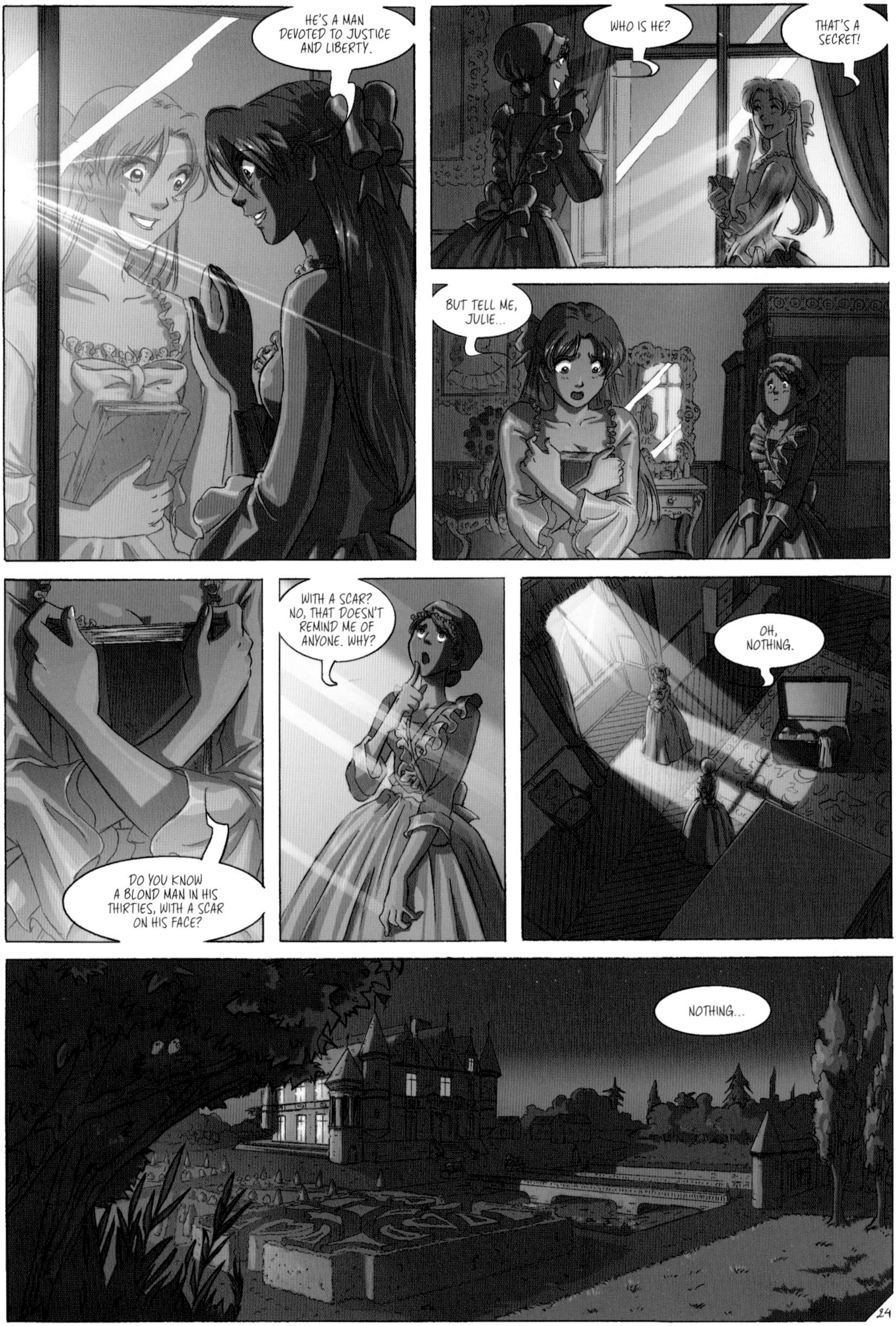
HE'S A MAN DEVOTED TO JUSTICE AND LIBERTY.
WHO IS HE?
THAT'S A SECRET!
BUT TELL ME, JULIE...
DO YOU KNOW A BLOND MAN IN HIS THIRTIES, WITH A SCAR ON HIS FACE?
WITH A SCAR? NO, THAT DOESN'T REMIND ME OF ANYONE. WHY?
OH, NOTHING.
NOTHING...
24

THUS DID MAUD BEGIN HER LIFE AT THE CASTLE WITH HER TEACHERS...

25

29

I WON'T STAY HERE ONE MINUTE LONGER! YOUR GRANDDAUGHTER IS A SAVAGE WHO ONLY WANTS TO RIDE HORSES!

AND SHE PREFERS SWORDPLAY TO POETRY!

WE'D RATHER LEAVE! GOODBYE, YOUR LORDSHIP!

I HOPE YOU'RE PROUD OF YOURSELF. YOUR NEW TEACHERS JUST STORMED OUT.

THAT'S THE FOURTH TIME THIS MONTH.

IF THEY'D TEACH ME FENCING, IT WOULD BE DIFFERENT.

I'M TAKING YOU TO THE DUKE DE LA VOLIERE'S ANNUAL BALL TOMORROW EVENING. I WON'T ALLOW ANY MISCONDUCT AND WILL FIND YOU A GOOD MATCH.

BUT--?

MILORD, YOU HAVE A VISITOR.

?!

26

I'M SERGEANT DRAULT OF THE CONSTABULARY.

EXCUSE ME FOR INTERRUPTING YOUR DINNER, BUT "THE FOX" HAS ATTACKED A COUPLE IN A CARRIAGE NEARBY.

WE'D LIKE TO SURROUND YOUR LANDS TO CAPTURE HIM.

THE FOX? THAT BANDIT?!

THE FOX?!

PLEASE DO, SERGEANT. I'LL PUT MY MEN AT YOUR DISPOSAL.

THANK YOU, MILORD.

OH, HOW STRANGE. I DON'T FEEL GOOD...

CLACK

WHAT'S WRONG?

BURP!

I FEEL A LITTLE INDISPOSED.

GO REST SO YOU'LL BE BETTER BY TOMORROW NIGHT.

OOOO...

27

MADEMOISELLE, WHAT ARE YOU DOING?

THE FOX! I MUST WARN HIM! THE SOLDIERS ARE LAYING A TRAP FOR HIM HERE. I MUST FIND HIM AND TELL HIM TO GO ANOTHER WAY!

DON'T WORRY, JULIE! PLEASE COVER FOR ME, I'M SUPPOSED TO BE ILL!

BUT...

SHH, COMET. WE'RE GOING TO TAKE A LITTLE NOCTURNAL RIDE!

HOP

I MUST FIND HIM BEFORE THEY DO!

WHAT'S WRONG, COMET?

OH, NO, YOU'VE HURT YOUR LEG.

WAIT FOR ME HERE. I'LL GO ASK THAT FARMER FOR SOMETHING TO MAKE YOU A DRESSING.

AAAH!

SPLASH

OINK?

EEEEE!

OH, NO, THIS CAN'T BE HAPPENING!

HEY!

29

BOOM
BOOM

OH!
QUICK!

PLEASE!
STOP!

WHOA!

WELL, WHAT
DO YOU WISH OF
ME, MADEMOISELLE?
HAVING A MIDNIGHT
BATH?

UH, UHM...
YOU MUST SKIRT THE
LANDS OF THE COUNT OF
LAROCHE. SOME SOLDIERS
MEAN TO CAPTURE YOU,
MONSIEUR FOX!

30

WHY ARE YOU HELPING ME, MADEMOISELLE? YOU KNOW I'M A BRIGAND.

BECAUSE THOUSANDS OF PEOPLE NEED YOU! BELIEVE ME, I BEG YOU! GO THE OTHER WAY!

...

VERY WELL, IF IT WOULD PLEASE SUCH A CHARMING APPARITION! FAREWELL!

IT'S HORRIBLE. I FINALLY MEET HIM...

...HERE AMONG THE PIGS.

31

THE NEXT EVENING, AT THE CASTLE OF THE DUKE DE LA VOLIERE...

MAUD, I INSIST THAT YOU BEHAVE.

NO SCANDALS TONIGHT!

YES, YES!

THE COUNT DE LAROCHE AND MADEMOISELLE DE LAROCHE.

!?

OOOOOH!

OH, MY GOD, WHY, SHE'S A TRAMP!

HOW DARE YOU?

YOU WANTED ME TO COME, SO I CAME!

32

?!

I'LL HAVE A LITTLE FUN, TOO!

GOOD EVENING!

HEE HEE HEE

HOW INDECENT TO DRESS SO! THAT DRESS IS WRETCHED!

EXACTLY!

?!

UH...

BLABLABLA BLABLABLABLABLA BLABLABLA!

HAHAHA!

AH, THOSE NOBLES! HOW DREADFUL!

I HOPE THAT, AFTER THIS ENTIRE CIRCUS, HE WON'T EVER TRY TO MAKE ME GO TO ONE OF THESE SOIREES AGAIN!

PERSONALLY, I THOUGHT YOU WERE PERFECT!

33

?!

I DON'T CARE TO MAKE ANY FRIENDS, MONSIEUR, SO LEAVE, PLEASE.

YOU'RE QUITE CHARMING, AND YOUR GRANDFATHER IS LIVID!

YOU PULLED IT OFF PERFECTLY! BRAVO!

ALL THE BETTER THEN. TO WHOM DO I HAVE THE HONOR?

MY NAME IS GUILHEM, COUNT OF LANDREY. I SEE THAT, LIKE ME, YOU DON'T MUCH LIKE THIS SORT OF SHOW.

OH, I HATE THEM ALL. THERE THEY ARE, STRUTTING AROUND IN FINERY WHILE SO MANY PEOPLE ARE SUFFERING!

YOU'RE PERFECTLY CORRECT.

BUT THEN, WHY ARE YOU HERE?

I COME ONLY BECAUSE I'M FORCED TO, JUST LIKE YOU.

REALLY?

I'D PREFER TO SPEND MY TIME RIDING. THIS EVENING WAS A BORE BEFORE YOU ARRIVED. ALTHOUGH A FEW LADIES FAINTED, YOUR DRESS IS MAGNIFICENT.

34

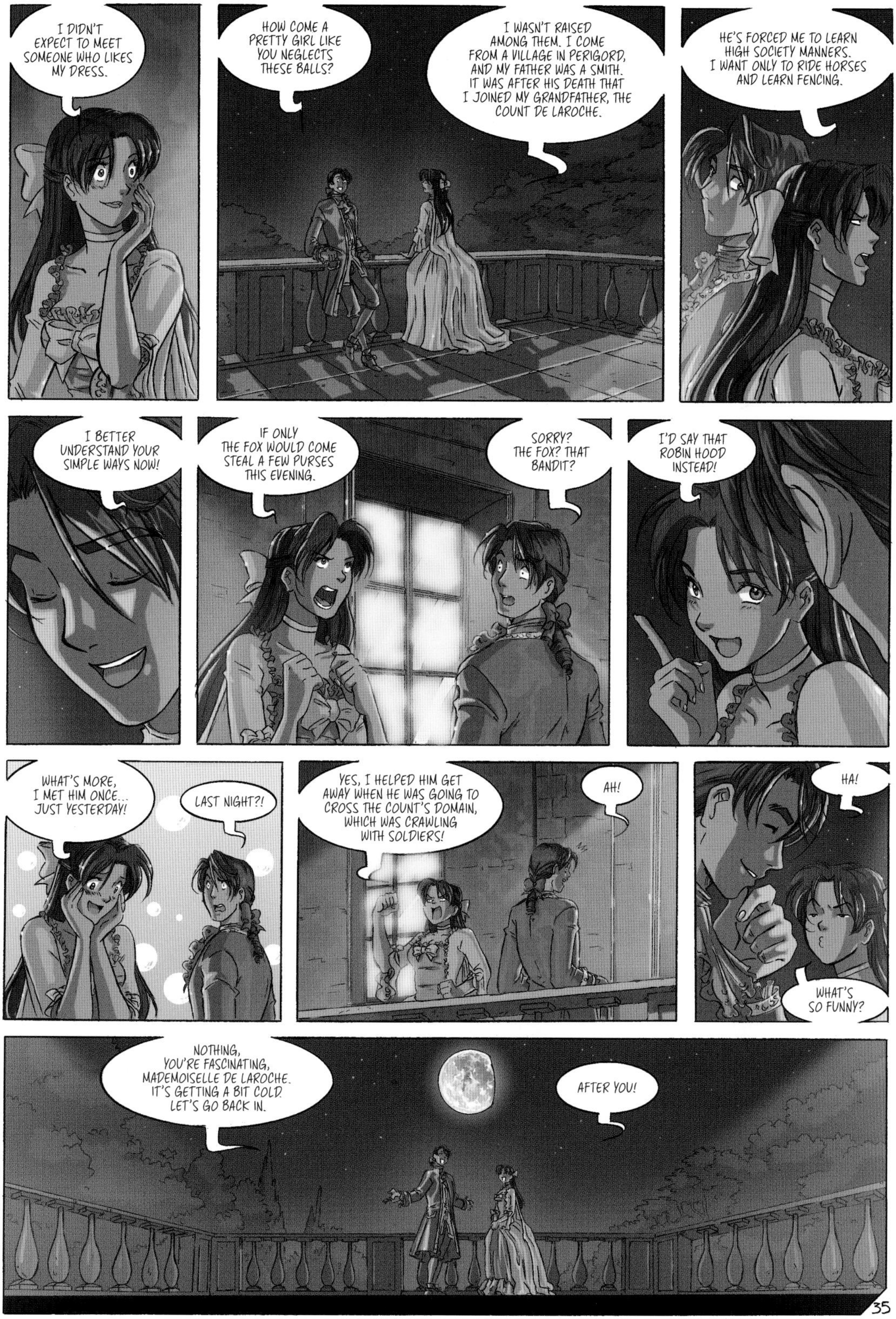
I DIDN'T EXPECT TO MEET SOMEONE WHO LIKES MY DRESS.
HOW COME A PRETTY GIRL LIKE YOU NEGLECTS THESE BALLS?
I WASN'T RAISED AMONG THEM. I COME FROM A VILLAGE IN PERIGORD, AND MY FATHER WAS A SMITH. IT WAS AFTER HIS DEATH THAT I JOINED MY GRANDFATHER, THE COUNT DE LAROCHE.
HE'S FORCED ME TO LEARN HIGH SOCIETY MANNERS. I WANT ONLY TO RIDE HORSES AND LEARN FENCING.
I BETTER UNDERSTAND YOUR SIMPLE WAYS NOW!
IF ONLY THE FOX WOULD COME STEAL A FEW PURSES THIS EVENING.
SORRY? THE FOX? THAT BANDIT?
I'D SAY THAT ROBIN HOOD INSTEAD!
WHAT'S MORE, I MET HIM ONCE... JUST YESTERDAY!
LAST NIGHT?!
YES, I HELPED HIM GET AWAY WHEN HE WAS GOING TO CROSS THE COUNT'S DOMAIN, WHICH WAS CRAWLING WITH SOLDIERS!
AH!
HA!
WHAT'S SO FUNNY?
NOTHING, YOU'RE FASCINATING, MADEMOISELLE DE LAROCHE. IT'S GETTING A BIT COLD. LET'S GO BACK IN.
AFTER YOU!
35

WHY...
THAT FACE?!

IT'S
YOU!

YOU KILLED
MY FATHER!

?!

AAAAA

AAAAH

BUT IT'S
IMPOSSIBLE!

THE SCAR! THERE SHOULD
BE A SCAR THERE!

36

40

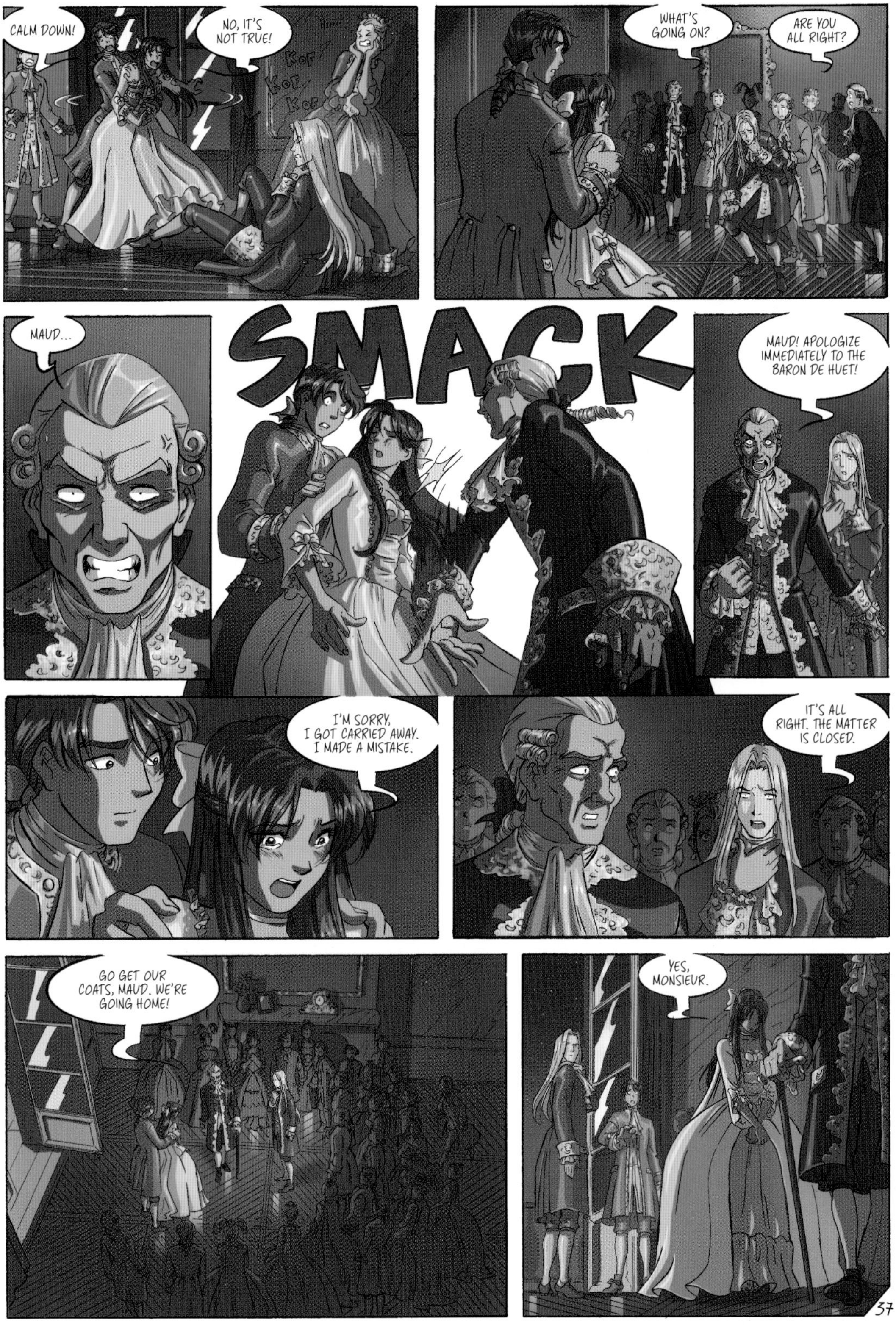
CALM DOWN!
NO, IT'S NOT TRUE!
KOF KOF KOF
WHAT'S GOING ON?
ARE YOU ALL RIGHT?
MAUD...
SMACK
MAUD! APOLOGIZE IMMEDIATELY TO THE BARON DE HUET!
I'M SORRY, I GOT CARRIED AWAY. I MADE A MISTAKE.
IT'S ALL RIGHT. THE MATTER IS CLOSED.
GO GET OUR COATS, MAUD. WE'RE GOING HOME!
YES, MONSIEUR.
37

WELL, THAT YOUNG LADY IS A BIT ECCENTRIC!

YES, WHAT STRANGE BEHAVIOR TOWARDS THE BARON.

HMM, SHE'S QUITE YOUNG. DON'T DECEIVE HER, COUNT.

I WASN'T EVEN THINKING OF THAT, MARQUISE. AT THE MOMENT, YOU'RE THE ONE I DON'T WISH TO DECEIVE.

LITTLE SCAMP!

HENCEFORTH, MAUD, YOU WILL STAY SHUT UP AT THE CASTLE! YOU'VE CREATED ENOUGH SCANDALS FOR ONE NIGHT!

YES.

IT WAS HIM, I'M SURE OF IT! HE HAD THE SAME VOICE, THE SAME FACE!

BUT WHY DIDN'T HE HAVE A SCAR?

38

MADEMOISELLE! THE COUNT DESIRES YOU TO JOIN HIM IN THE BIG SITTING ROOM.

TGLAC

?!

MAUD, I PRESENT TO YOU THE COUNT DE LANDREY, WHO PROPOSES TO BE YOUR FENCING TEACHER.

HELLO, MAUD.

REALLY?

39

AFTER THE OTHER EVENING'S SCANDAL, I THOUGHT NOBODY WOULD SPEAK TO YOU AGAIN, BUT THE COUNT INSISTED ON SEEING YOU. HE'LL HELP YOU.

THANK YOU, MILORD!

CALL ME GUILHEM.

TAKE NOTE, I'LL BE A DEMANDING TEACHER!

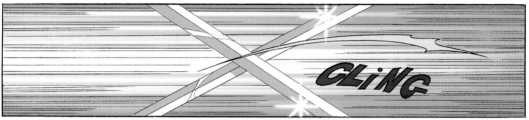

CLING

MAUD IS SEEING THAT YOUNG COUNT?

NO, HE'S HER FENCING TEACHER. THE COUNT DE LANDREY HAS A RATHER DUBIOUS REPUTATION.

HE'S A DON JUAN, AND I DON'T WANT HER FALLING IN LOVE WITH HIM.

WELL!

40

YOU'RE MUCH BETTER THAN I IMAGINED!

MY FATHER TAUGHT ME EVERYTHING HE KNEW.

I'D LIKE TO KNOW, THE OTHER NIGHT, YOU ACCUSED THE BARON DE HUET OF MURDER.

!?

!?

I DON'T UNDERSTAND, HE HAS THE SAME FACE AS MY FATHER'S KILLER...

...EXCEPTING A SCAR.

WHAT'S THE BARON LIKE?

WELL, HE'S A SOCIETY MAN.

IT'S STRANGE.

TO TELL THE TRUTH, I DOUBT HE'S YOUR FATHER'S ASSASSIN. HE NEVER LEAVES PARIS AND IS PRESENT AT ALL THE SOCIETY PARTIES IN THE AREA.

41

SO, SMILE FOR ME!

TELL ME OF YOUR PASSION FOR THE FOX!

IT'S NOT VERY FITTING FOR A YOUNG LADY OF YOUR RANK TO ADMIRE A BANDIT! WHAT WOULD YOUR GRANDFATHER SAY?

I'LL TRY TO FIND OUT ABOUT THE BARON. WE'LL FIND YOUR FATHER'S ASSASSIN.

HIS OPINION IS OF LITTLE IMPORT TO ME. THE FOX FASCINATES ME. HE HAS DREAMS AND MAKES THEM COME TRUE.

AND WHAT DO YOU KNOW OF HIS DREAMS?

I KNOW HE WANTS A FAIRER WORLD AND FIGHTS TO HELP THE POOR.

AND HOW ARE YOU SO SURE OF THAT?

I KNOW SO, THAT'S ALL!

CLING

SIII

OWW!

STAC

AND WHY DON'T YOU FULFILL YOUR DREAMS?

YOU'RE GROWN UP! YOU CAN DO WHAT YOU LIKE!

42

?!

JULIE? WHERE'S THE ATTIC?

AAH!

EXACTLY WHAT I WAS LOOKING FOR! JULIE, YOU'LL HAVE TO HELP ME SEW TONIGHT!

43

THERE! ALL I NEED NOW IS A MASK!
MADEMOISELLE, WON'T THIS BE A LITTLE DANGEROUS?
NO! YOU JUST HAVE TO HAVE CONFIDENCE!
WHAT DO YOU THINK, JULIE?
FROM NOW ON, THEY'LL CALL ME "SCARLET"!
I'LL DEFEND WIDOWS AND ORPHANS AND DISPENSE JUSTICE!
OH, YES!
BUT BEFORE ALL THAT, I MUST FIND MY FATHER'S KILLER! I'M SURE HE MUST BE HIDING AMONG THE BANDITS OF PARIS!
44

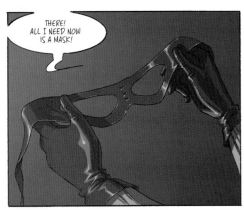

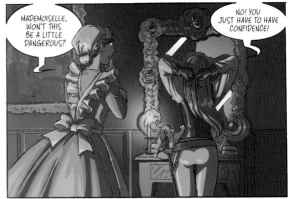

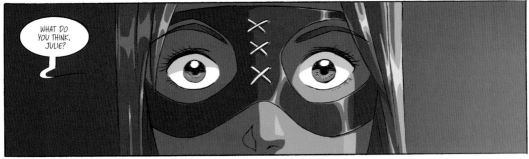

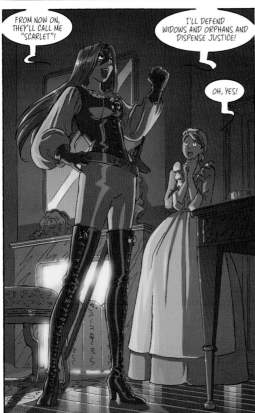

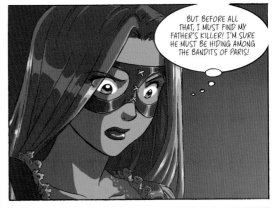

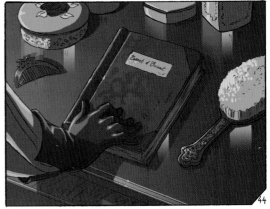

HEY! YOU COMING UP, HANDSOME?

HEE HEE HEE!

WHOA!

ALL RIGHT, THE NIGHT'S OVER FOR YOU, YOUNG BARONET!

COME SEE US AGAIN MORE OFTEN!

SEE YOU SOON, YOU LOVELY WILD FLOWERS! →HIC← I'LL COME PLUCK YOU AGAIN! →HIC←

45

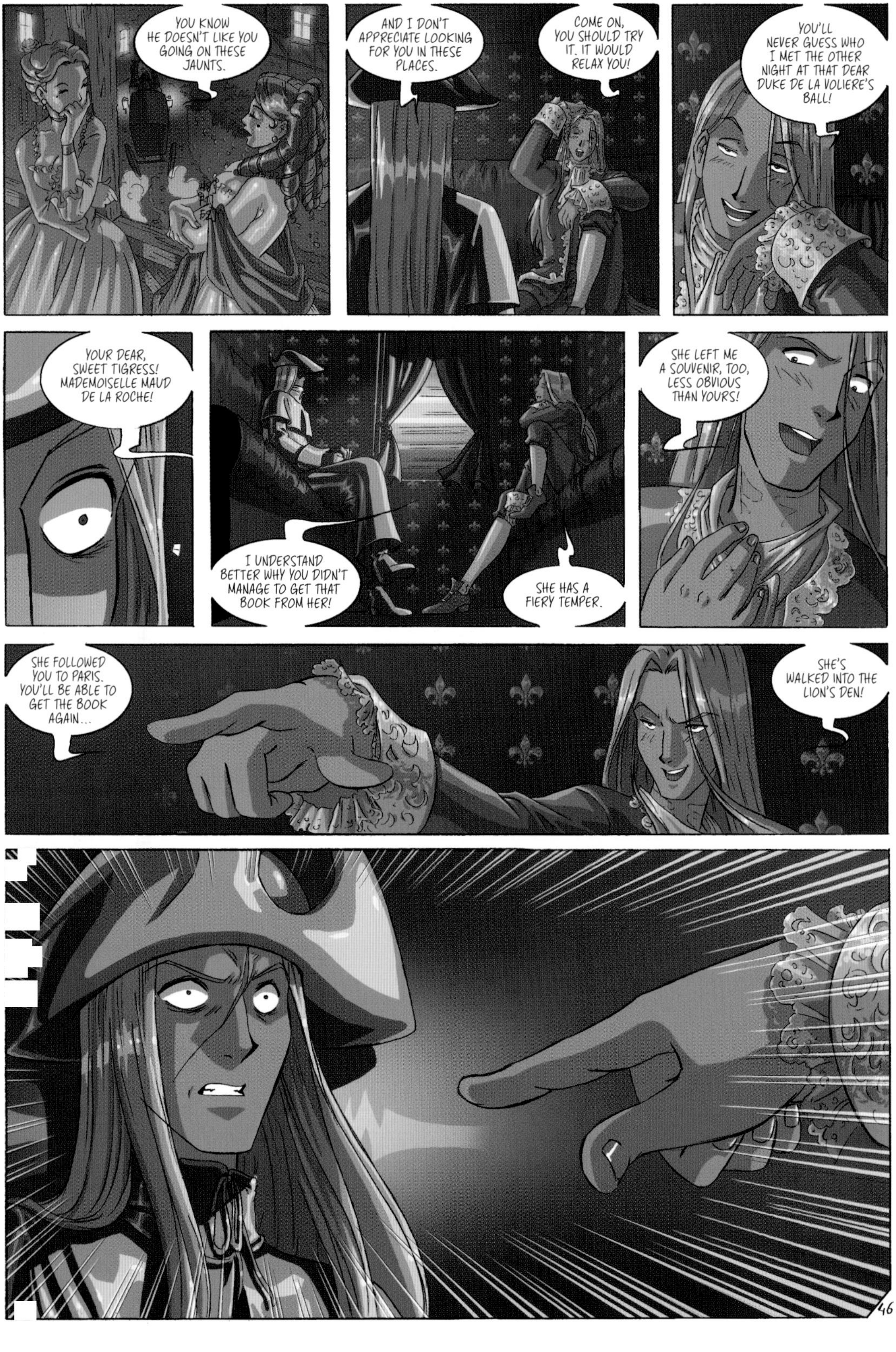
YOU KNOW HE DOESN'T LIKE YOU GOING ON THESE JAUNTS.
AND I DON'T APPRECIATE LOOKING FOR YOU IN THESE PLACES.
COME ON, YOU SHOULD TRY IT. IT WOULD RELAX YOU!
YOU'LL NEVER GUESS WHO I MET THE OTHER NIGHT AT THAT DEAR DUKE DE LA VOLIERE'S BALL!
YOUR DEAR, SWEET TIGRESS! MADEMOISELLE MAUD DE LA ROCHE!
I UNDERSTAND BETTER WHY YOU DIDN'T MANAGE TO GET THAT BOOK FROM HER!
SHE HAS A FIERY TEMPER.
SHE LEFT ME A SOUVENIR, TOO, LESS OBVIOUS THAN YOURS!
SHE FOLLOWED YOU TO PARIS. YOU'LL BE ABLE TO GET THE BOOK AGAIN...
SHE'S WALKED INTO THE LION'S DEN!
46

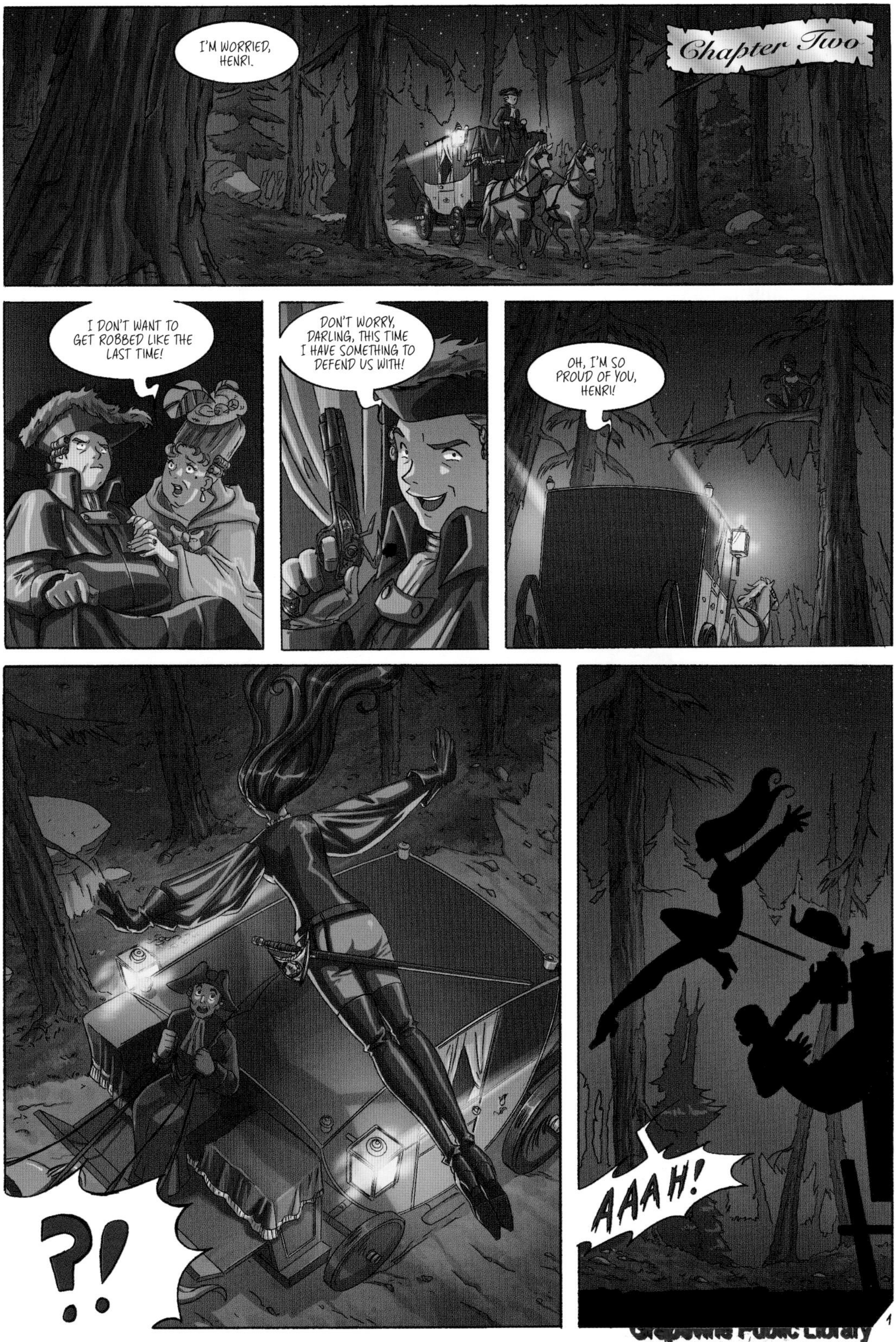
Chapter Two
I'M WORRIED, HENRI.
I DON'T WANT TO GET ROBBED LIKE THE LAST TIME!
DON'T WORRY, DARLING, THIS TIME I HAVE SOMETHING TO DEFEND US WITH!
OH, I'M SO PROUD OF YOU, HENRI!
?!
AAAH!

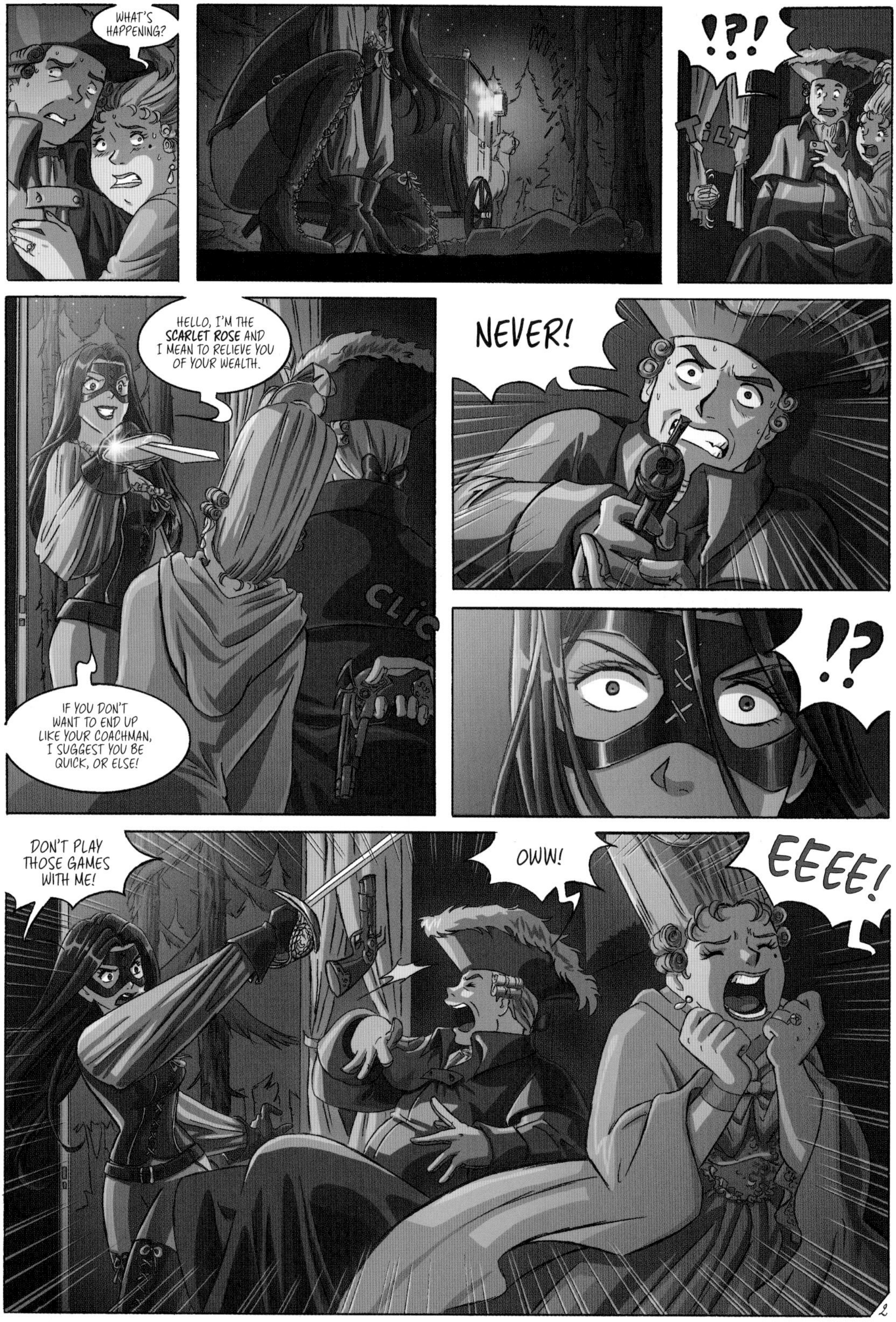
WHAT'S HAPPENING?
!?!
TILT
HELLO, I'M THE **SCARLET ROSE** AND I MEAN TO RELIEVE YOU OF YOUR WEALTH.
IF YOU DON'T WANT TO END UP LIKE YOUR COACHMAN, I SUGGEST YOU BE QUICK, OR ELSE!
CLIC
NEVER!
!?
DON'T PLAY THOSE GAMES WITH ME!
OWW!
EEEE!
2

YOUR PURSE AND YOUR JEWELS!

YES, RIGHT AWAY.

AND IF YOU CROSS PATHS WITH MY COLLEAGUE THE FOX, ONE DAY...

...TELL HIM THE SCARLET ROSE IS LOOKING FOR HIM!

FAREWELL.

A RIDER, AT THIS TIME OF THE NIGHT?

?!

GOD IN HEAVEN! IT'S A FORTUNE FOR THE CHILDREN!

3

HAVE YOU HEARD? IT SEEMS A NOBLEMAN'S CARRIAGE WAS ATTACKED BY A MASKED YOUNG WOMAN...

...WHO'S CALLING HERSELF THE SCARLET ROSE!

Wanted

1,000 Crowns

SHE MOCKED THEM, THEN TOOK THEIR MONEY AND JEWELS AND GAVE IT ALL TO THE ORPHANAGE OF THE LITTLE ANGELS.

YES, NOW THE LITTLE PEOPLE CAN COUNT ON HER AND THE FOX!

LET'S HOPE THE CONSTABULARY NEVER CATCHES THEM!

YOU SEEM TO BE IN GOOD FORM, MAUD.

YES, I'M VERY HAPPY AT THE MOMENT!

IN ANY CASE, YOU'VE MADE A LOT OF PROGRESS OF LATE.

ARE YOU TRAINING IN SECRET?

NO, YOU'RE AN ESPECIALLY GOOD TEACHER.

4

GUILHEM, HAVE YOU LEARNED ANYTHING ABOUT THE BARON DE HUET?

YES, I'VE DONE MY INVESTIGATION DISCREETLY.

HIS NAME IS ALBERT DE HUET AND HE WAS ADOPTED AT THE AGE OF TEN BY THE OLD BARON WHO HAD NEITHER A WIFE NOR DESCENDANTS.

ALBERT WAS THE SON OF ONE OF HIS SERVANT-GIRLS.

"DESPITE HIS MODEST ORIGINS, HE HAS MANAGED TO ESTABLISH HIMSELF IN HIGH SOCIETY THANKS TO HIS CHARISMA. UPON THE OLD MADMAN'S DEATH, HE INHERITED THE TITLE AND THE LANDS."

THE "OLD MADMAN"?

YES, THAT'S WHAT THE OLD BARON WAS NICKNAMED.

THEY SAID HE WAS MAD BECAUSE, HIS WHOLE LIFE, HE SEARCHED FOR THE SECRET OF THE TEMPLARS, THOSE KNIGHT-MONKS OF THE MIDDLE AGES.

"SEVERAL TIMES HE DEPARTED ON EXPEDITIONS TO THE ORIENT TO UNCOVER THEIR SECRETS, BUT NEVER FOUND IT. AND I THINK THAT IT KILLED HIM."

THE ORIENT? MY FATHER VISITED THE ORIENT, TOO!

YES, YES!

COME, GUILHEM, I'LL SHOW YOU!

5

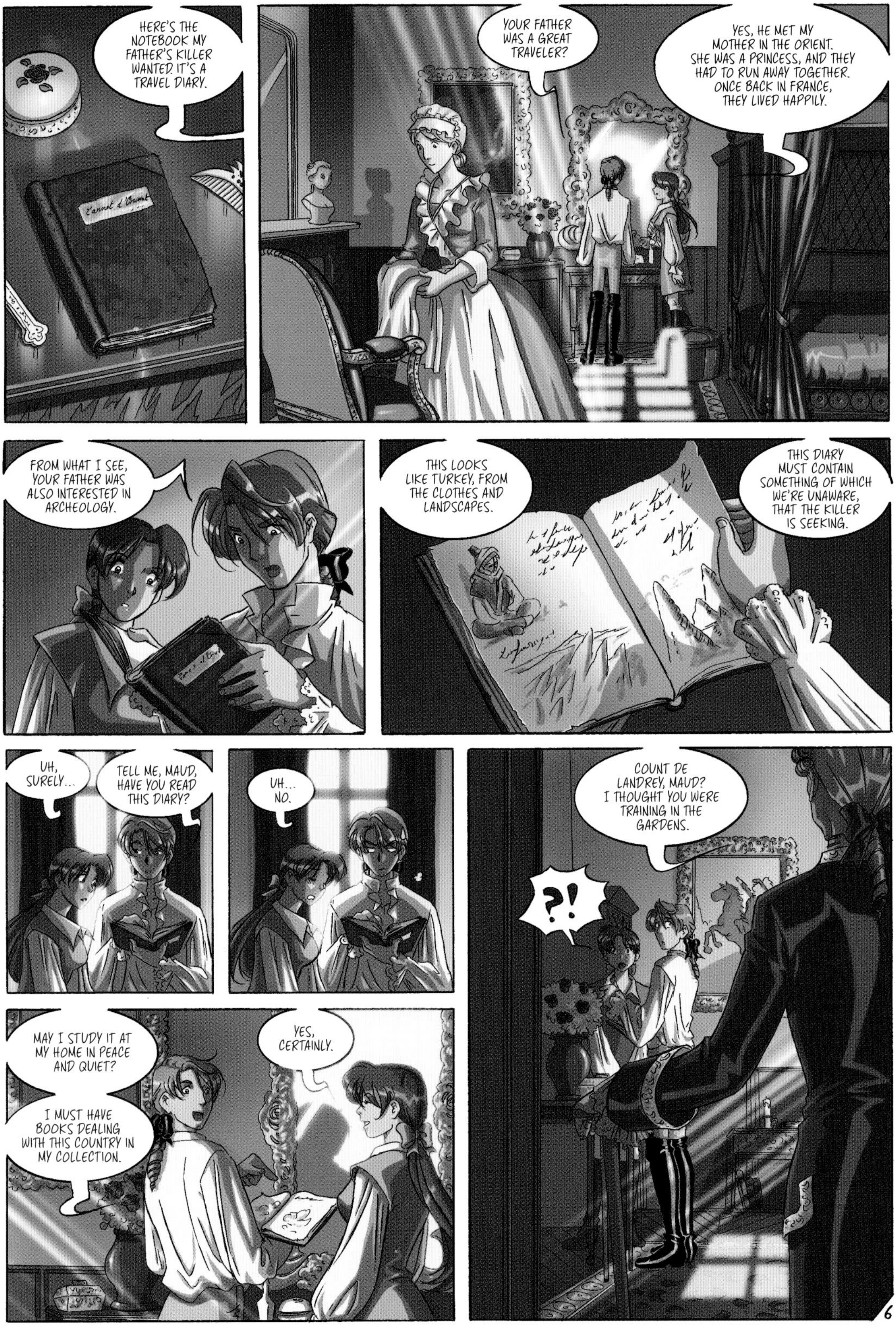
HERE'S THE NOTEBOOK MY FATHER'S KILLER WANTED. IT'S A TRAVEL DIARY.
Carnet d'Orient
YOUR FATHER WAS A GREAT TRAVELER?
YES, HE MET MY MOTHER IN THE ORIENT. SHE WAS A PRINCESS, AND THEY HAD TO RUN AWAY TOGETHER. ONCE BACK IN FRANCE, THEY LIVED HAPPILY.
FROM WHAT I SEE, YOUR FATHER WAS ALSO INTERESTED IN ARCHEOLOGY.
THIS LOOKS LIKE TURKEY, FROM THE CLOTHES AND LANDSCAPES.
THIS DIARY MUST CONTAIN SOMETHING OF WHICH WE'RE UNAWARE, THAT THE KILLER IS SEEKING.
TELL ME, MAUD, HAVE YOU READ THIS DIARY?
UH, SURELY...
UH... NO.
MAY I STUDY IT AT MY HOME IN PEACE AND QUIET?
I MUST HAVE BOOKS DEALING WITH THIS COUNTRY IN MY COLLECTION.
YES, CERTAINLY.
COUNT DE LANDREY, MAUD? I THOUGHT YOU WERE TRAINING IN THE GARDENS.
?!
6

UHM, I--

MAUD WAS SHOWING ME HER COLLECTION OF BROOCHES!

IT'S OF NO IMPORTANCE. I'VE JUST RECEIVED AN INVITATION TO THE BARON DE HUET'S TOMORROW EVENING.

YOU'RE ALSO INVITED, COUNT DE LANDREY.

BUT WHY?

MAYBE HE'S NOT RESENTFUL ABOUT WHAT YOU DID TO HIM.

I DON'T WANT TO.

I'LL BE THERE. DON'T WORRY, MAUD.

COUNT DE LANDREY, I'D LIKE TO CHAT A FEW MOMENTS WITH YOU.

7

YOU ENJOY A GOOD RELATIONSHIP WITH MY GRANDDAUGHTER, FROM WHAT I SEE.

TO BE BLUNT, I DISTRUST YOU. YOUR REPUTATION ISN'T THE MOST PRAISEWORTHY.

YES, I THINK SO.

YOU'RE, HOWEVER, THE ONLY ONE WHO SEEMS TO HAVE GAINED MAUD'S TRUST.

MAUD AND I CAN'T STOP ARGUING. I ADMIT TO NOT BEHAVING WELL, BUT I'M VERY FOND OF HER.

I HAVE A FAVOR TO ASK OF YOU. WOULD YOU HELP ME GAIN HER TRUST?

...IT WOULD BE MY PLEASURE AND A TRUE HONOR!

DEAR COUNT...

THE NEXT EVENING, AT THE CASTLE OF THE BARON DE HUET...

GOOD EVENING. I'LL TAKE YOUR CLOAKS, PLEASE.

THERE ARE MY GUESTS, INCLUDING THAT DEAR MAUD DE LAROCHE.

HMM, SHE IS MOST CHARMING.

FRESH AND PURE AS A ROSEBUD.

?!

59

I FORBID YOU TO TOUCH HER, DO YOU HEAR? SHE'S MINE!

CALM DOWN, ALBAN! SO BE IT, SHE'S YOURS!

WELL, I MUST RECEIVE MY GUESTS, I'LL LEAVE YOU TO YOUR DIRTY WORK.

WELCOME, MY DEAR FRIENDS!

I'M DELIGHTED YOU ACCEPTED MY INVITATION TO DINNER.

GOOD EVENING, BARON. PLEASE ACCEPT MY APOLOGIES WITH RESPECT TO THE INCIDENT AT THE DUKE DE LA VOLIERE'S HOME.

CALL ME ALBERT, I BEG YOU. YOU'RE HERE TONIGHT, AND ALL IS FORGIVEN.

FOLLOW ME. THE TABLE IS ALREADY SET.

?!

IT'LL BE FINE!

10

THANK YOU FOR FORGIVING MY GRANDDAUGHTER'S UNFORTUNATE DEED, BARON.

SHE CONFUSED ME WITH HER FATHER'S KILLER, THAT'S OBVIOUS.

WELL...

I'VE ALWAYS HAD PROBLEMS WITH MY SIGHT. I WAS MISTAKEN, I'M SORRY!

I'M SO ASHAMED OF HER BEHAVIOR, I--

NO, NO, IT'S NOTHING.

TELL ME, ALBERT, DO YOU TRAVEL MUCH?

NO, NEVER. TRAVEL DRIVES ME MAD, TO BE HONEST. I'M VERY HAPPY AT HOME SURROUNDED BY MY FRIENDS HERE. WHY WOULD I LEAVE?

OH, IT'S THE SAME FOR ME! I HAVE A PASSION FOR FENCING. AND YOU, ALBERT, DO YOU PRACTICE THE ART?

NO, I'M THE LAZIEST MAN IN THE WORLD. I LEAVE IT TO COUNT DE LANDREY, IT'S TOO VIOLENT FOR MY TASTES.

THE ONLY THING I'M PASSIONATE ABOUT I INHERITED FROM MY LATE, ADOPTIVE FATHER. MY DEAR MAUD, DO YOU KNOW ABOUT THE TEMPLARS?

HIS WHOLE LIFE, MY FATHER SOUGHT TO REVEAL THEIR TREASURE, BUT IN VAIN. THOSE KNIGHT-MONKS HID IT SOMEWHERE BETWEEN FRANCE AND JERUSALEM.

WELL, MAYBE THAT SECRET WAS SIMPLY THEIR FAITH.

HA HA HA HA!

WHAT A DELIGHTFUL RESPONSE! YOU'RE CHARMING, MAUD!

12

62

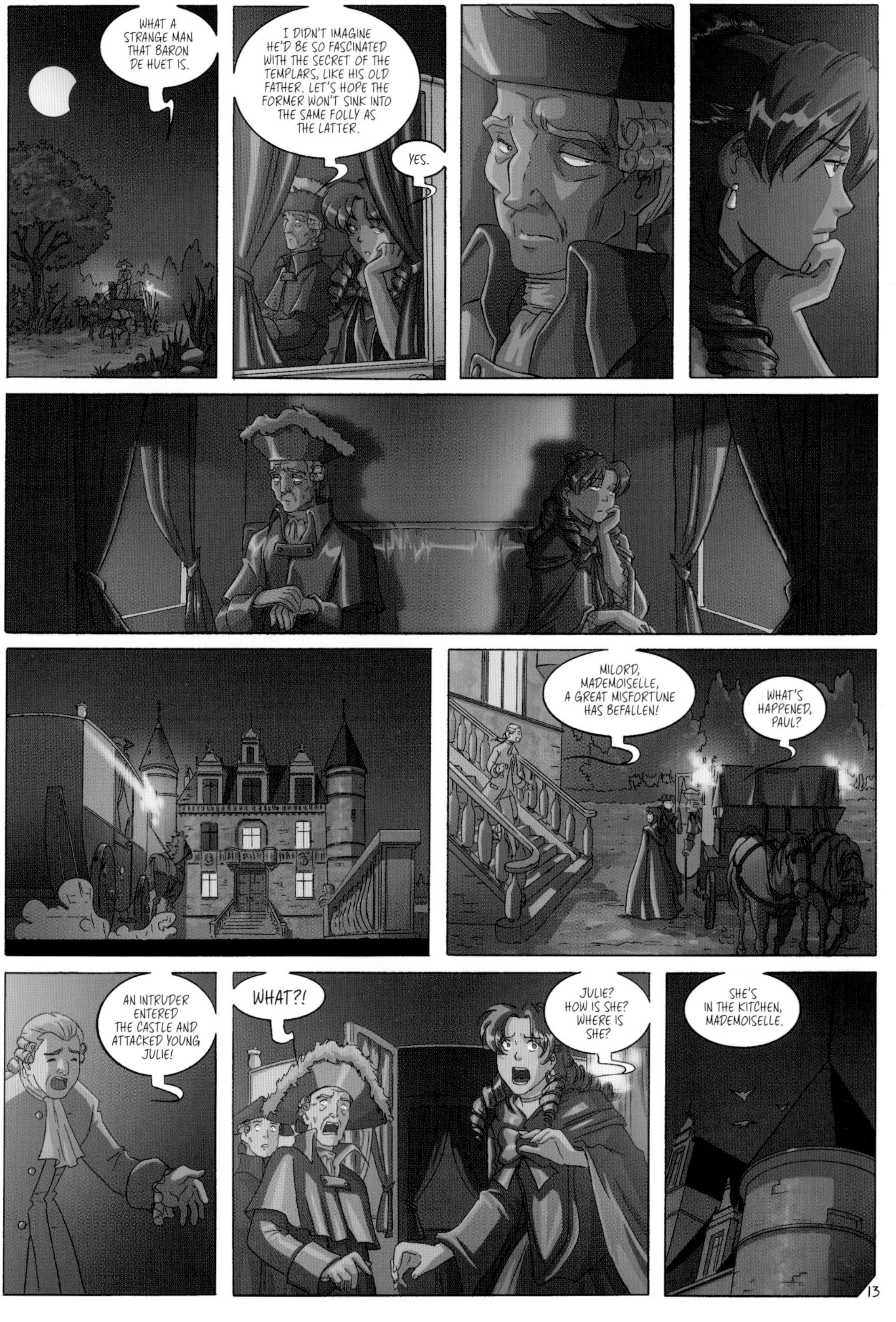
WHAT A STRANGE MAN THAT BARON DE HUET IS.
I DIDN'T IMAGINE HE'D BE SO FASCINATED WITH THE SECRET OF THE TEMPLARS, LIKE HIS OLD FATHER. LET'S HOPE THE FORMER WON'T SINK INTO THE SAME FOLLY AS THE LATTER.
YES.
MILORD, MADEMOISELLE, A GREAT MISFORTUNE HAS BEFALLEN!
WHAT'S HAPPENED, PAUL?
AN INTRUDER ENTERED THE CASTLE AND ATTACKED YOUNG JULIE!
WHAT?!
JULIE? HOW IS SHE? WHERE IS SHE?
SHE'S IN THE KITCHEN, MADEMOISELLE.
13

JULIE, HOW ARE YOU?

I'M BETTER, THANKS. MADEMOISELLE MAUD, A BANDIT WAS LOOKING FOR YOUR FATHER'S NOTEBOOK.

HE THREATENED TO KILL ME, IF I DIDN'T TELL HIM WHERE IT WAS.

MY FATHER'S NOTEBOOK? IT WAS HIS KILLER! DID HE HAVE A SCAR IN THE MIDDLE OF HIS FACE?

I DON'T KNOW. HE WAS MASKED.

WE WERE AT THE BARON'S TONIGHT. IT CAN'T BE HIM.

AND DID YOU TELL HIM THE COUNT DE LANDREY HAD THE NOTEBOOK?

YES, I'M SORRY. THEN THE BRIGAND DISAPPEARED.

IT'S ALL RIGHT, JULIE. THE IMPORTANT THING IS THAT YOU'RE SAFE AND SOUND.

I'LL TELL GUILHEM TO BE CAREFUL WITH THE NOTEBOOK.

WHAT'S THIS ABOUT A NOTEBOOK?

OH, NO, IT'S NOTHING IMPORTANT.

I'M SURE THIS IS AN ATTACK BY THE FOX! I'LL HAVE HIM ARRESTED!

NO, IT'S NOT HIM! THE MAN WHO ATTACKED JULIE WAS AFTER ME! HE'S NOT THE FOX!

SO BE IT! THAT BANDIT WILL BE PUNISHED ONE DAY OR ANOTHER!

SLAM

JULIE, I'LL FIND YOUR ATTACKER, AND HE'LL PAY, BELIEVE ME!

14

IMBECILE! HOW IS THAT YOU CAN'T PROCURE A SIMPLE NOTEBOOK?

SHE GAVE IT TO THE COUNT DE LANDREY. I'LL GO GET IT FROM HIM.

YOU'D BETTER. THANKS TO THAT NOTEBOOK, WE'LL FINALLY BE ABLE TO REACH OUR GOAL.

I'LL GET IT THIS TIME!

AND THEN, I'LL PERSONALLY SEE TO THAT GUILHEM DE LANDREY.

15

IN THE MEANTIME, MAUD CONTINUES HER NOCTURNAL ESCAPADES, SOMETIMES TO THE DETRIMENT OF HER NORMAL LIFE...

16

66

BASH

IF YOU SEE THE FOX, TELL HIM THE SCARLET ROSE IS LOOKING FOR HIM!

HOP

ONE NIGHT, HOWEVER...

BOOM

?!

HELLO!

SOKK

HEEEEEE

HELLO, LADIES AND GENTLEMEN! COULD YOU ENTRUST ME WITH YOUR GOODS AND PURSES, PLEASE?

?!

GUARDS! SEIZE THAT WOMAN!

IN THE NAME OF THE KING, WE'RE ARRESTING YOU FOR THEFT, SCARLET BRIGAND!

YOU WON'T ESCAPE US!

TAKE HER ALIVE!

THERE'S TOO MANY!

YOU'RE SURROUNDED!

AAAAH!

I GOT YOU!!

LET ME GO, YOU PACK OF COWARDS!

THE SHREW'S A STRONG ONE!

YOU'RE DONE FOR, SCARLET ROSE!

GRRR...

LET'S SEE WHO'S HIDING BEHIND THIS MASK!

HEEEEE

?!

BASH

?!

THE FOX!

THE FOX?

WHAT LUCK! TONIGHT WE'LL CAPTURE THE TWO GREATEST BRIGANDS IN FRANCE, AND I'LL BE PROMOTED BY THE KING HIMSELF!

INSTEAD OF DAYDREAMING ABOUT IT, TRY TO CAPTURE ME INSTEAD!

GUARDS! SEIZE HIM--

POW

UH...

WELL, I'LL ARREST YOU MYSELF!

20

YAAAH!

CAPTAIN--

BOP

AAAH!

CURSE YOU, FOX!

HELLO, MONSIEUR FOX!

I'M THE SCARLET ROSE. I'VE BEEN WANTING TO SEE YOU AGAIN FOR SO LONG!

21

SNAP

FOR ME, YOU'RE THE GREATEST RIGHTER OF WRONGS! STEALING FROM THE RICH AND GIVING TO THE POOR!

TAKE ME ON AS AN APPRENTICE. I'LL DO EVERYTHING YOU ASK OF ME!

I KNOW YOUR REPUTATION AND I THINK THIS LIFE IS TOO DANGEROUS FOR A YOUNG WOMAN.

AN OUTLAW'S LIFE ISN'T RIGHT FOR A WOMAN.

BUT...

IF YOU WANT TO PLEASE ME, FIND A NICE HUSBAND AND MAKE BEAUTIFUL CHILDREN FOR HIM.

FAREWELL, MADEMOISELLE SCARLET ROSE!

GIDDY-UP, COMET!

72

HOW CAN YOU SAY THAT? YOU'RE MY HERO! I ADMIRE YOU!

DON'T FOLLOW ME! I'M NOT WHO YOU THINK I AM! LEAVE!

NEVER! NOW THAT I'VE FOUND YOU, I WON'T LET YOU GO!

SHE'S QUITE FEISTY AND CLINGY TO BOOT!

AAAAAH!

!?!

23

73

PLUFF

YOU'RE CRAZY! YOU WANT TO GET US KILLED?

>KOF KOF!<

I ASKED YOU TO STOP! UM, NOTHING'S WRONG, AT LEAST?

NO, LUCKILY THAT HAY BROKE OUR FALL. LET ME GO, NOW.

NO! DON'T LEAVE!

WAIT!

?!

I LOVE YOU!

?!!

THAT'S IMPOSSIBLE! YOU DON'T EVEN KNOW ME!

AND YET I DO! GIVE ME A CHANCE!

!

WE WERE MADE FOR ONE ANOTHER, I KNOW IT!

MY NAME IS
MAUD. I GIVE
YOU MY LIFE!

?!

YOU?

PLOP

YES, WE MET
ONCE IN UNFORTUNATE
CIRCUMSTANCES, I WASN'T
AT MY BEST...

...BUT NOW
I CAN HELP
YOU IN YOUR
MISSION!

NO, YOU
CAN'T! I, I--

WAIT!

MONSIEUR
FOX--

MY FEELINGS
ARE SINCERE.

I MUST DO SOMETHING. WHAT MAUD IS DOING IS WAY TOO DANGEROUS!

LET'S GO SEE HER GRANDFATHER, MY BRAVE TEMPEST!

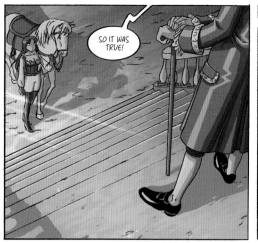

SO IT WAS TRUE!

I'M HARBORING A CRIMINAL IN MY HOME!

I'M NOT A CRIMINAL! I'M RIGHTING WRONGS!

MADEMOISELLE, I SWEAR TO YOU I NEVER BETRAYED YOU!

I KNOW, JULIE.

JULIE, YOU'RE DISMISSED!

?!

NO, I'M BEGGING YOU, MILORD!

AS FOR YOU, MAUD, I SHOULD REPORT YOU TO THE CONSTABULARY...

...BUT I HAVE A BETTER SOLUTION.

27

I AM SISTER BERNADETTE. I'M IN CHARGE OF THIS CONVENT.

IN THIS PLACE, PRAYER AND DISCIPLINE ARE THE ONLY RULES.

MAUD, YOU HAVE A HEADSTRONG NATURE, BUT WE'LL SEE THAT THAT CHANGES.

I'LL TAKE YOUR PERSONAL EFFECTS.

SISTER THERESA WILL GIVE YOU THE SCHEDULES FOR MEALS AND OFFICES...

CLIC

...AND I'LL HAVE YOU CONFESS YOUR SINS TO OUR LORD.

28

I'VE DONE NOTHING WRONG! THE LORD PROTECTS THE MOST WRETCHED, AND I DID EXACTLY THE SAME THING!

INSOLENT LITTLE THING! THANK YOUR GRANDFATHER FOR NOT DENOUNCING YOU! YOU SHOULD BE HANGING AT THE END OF A NOOSE RIGHT NOW!

SLAM

YOU'LL BEGIN WITH A DAY OF FASTING AND, TOMORROW, YOU WILL PRAY THE ENTIRE DAY.

SISTER THERESA, ACCOMPANY MADEMOISELLE DE LAROCHE TO HER CELL.

SLAM

THAT CHILD HAS QUITE AN ATTITUDE! BUT A BIT OF DISCIPLINE AND PRAYERS WILL SET HER ON THE RIGHT PATH AGAIN.

THANK YOU, SISTER.

I DON'T KNOW HOW TO DEAL WITH HER ANYMORE.

79

PUT ON THE DRESS THAT'S IN THE CHEST. I'LL COME BACK FOR YOURS.

A YOUNG MAN HAS COME TO PAY YOU A VISIT. IT WILL BE THE LAST ONE FOR A LONG TIME.

YOU HAVE TEN MINUTES.

GUILHEM! I'M HAPPY TO SEE YOU. HAVE YOU COME TO GET ME OUT OF HERE?

MY GRANDFATHER IS HORRIBLE! I DETEST HIM! HE'S DISMISSED JULIE, AND IT'S BECAUSE OF HIM I'M IN THIS CELL!

HE DISCOVERED THAT, WELL, YOU KNOW NOW, DON'T YOU?

YES, I KNOW. AND I UNDERSTAND WHY HE PUT YOU HERE.

WHY... ARE YOU ON HIS SIDE?

WHAT YOU DID, MAUD, IS VERY DANGEROUS!

A PRICE WAS PUT ON YOUR HEAD! THE COUNT IS TRYING TO PROTECT YOU IN HIS OWN WAY, OF COURSE.

I'D HAVE PREFERRED HE SIMPLY LOCKED YOU IN AT THE CASTLE.

30

WHY, YOU DENOUNCED ME! ADMIT IT! HOW DID YOU FIND OUT I WAS THE SCARLET ROSE?

UH, YOU LEFT YOUR COSTUME OUT IN YOUR BEDROOM.

BUT THAT'S IMPOSSIBLE. I ALWAYS PUT AWAY MY THINGS.

WHAT'S MORE, YOU'RE CONSTANTLY TIRED. I DEDUCED YOU HAD SOME NIGHTTIME ACTIVITY.

SO, YOU BETRAYED ME.

I HATE YOU! I'M STUCK IN THIS HOLE BECAUSE OF YOU!

MAUD, I NEVER WANTED THIS! BE CALM FOR A WHILE AND YOU'LL BE ABLE TO COME OUT AGAIN.

...

GO AWAY!

BOO-HOO

MAUD...

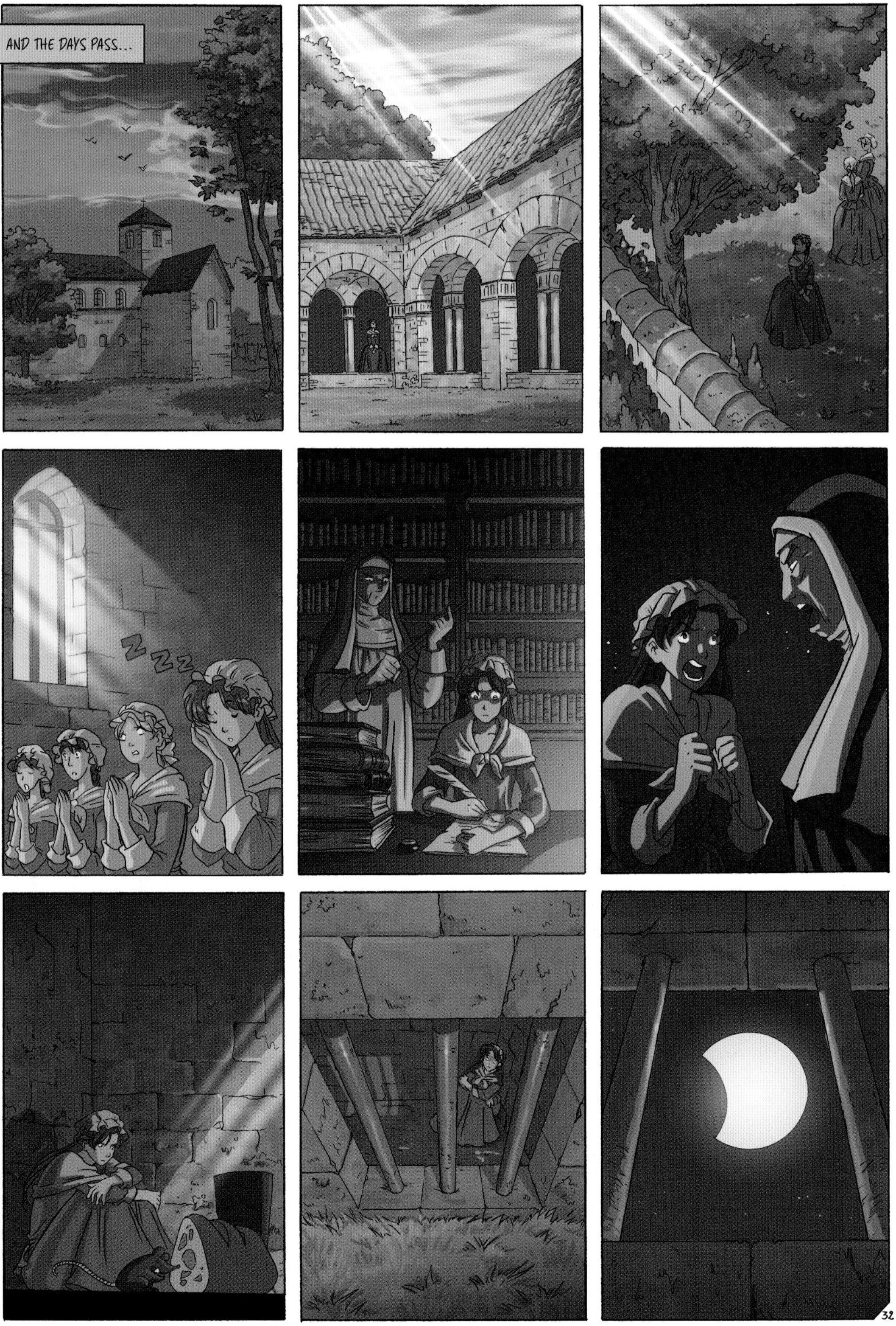
AND THE DAYS PASS...
ZZZ
32

AND THEN, ONE NIGHT...

LUCKILY, MY FRIEND PAUL TAUGHT ME A FEW LITTLE THIEF TRICKS!

33

83

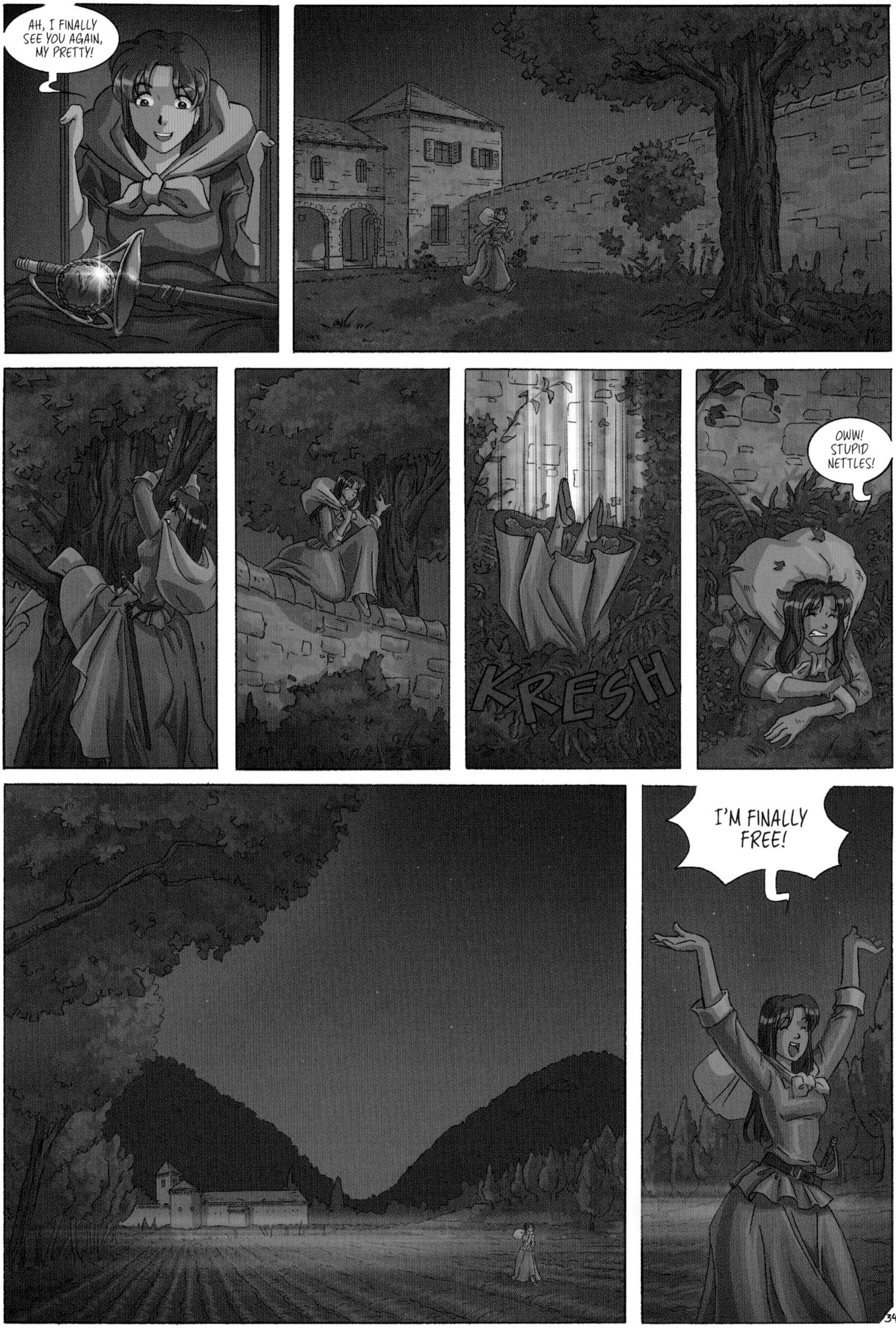
AH, I FINALLY SEE YOU AGAIN, MY PRETTY!
KRESH
OWW! STUPID NETTLES!
I'M FINALLY FREE!
34

ALL RIGHT. NOW I MUST FIND A CLOSE BY VILLAGE!

?

AH, I DON'T EVEN ENJOY RIGHTING WRONGS ANYMORE BECAUSE OF THIS.

HEEEEEE!

AAAH!

MAYBE I SHOULDN'T HAVE SPOKEN TO HER GRANDFATHER. SHE'D STILL BE FREE RIGHT NOW.

AAAH!

?

35

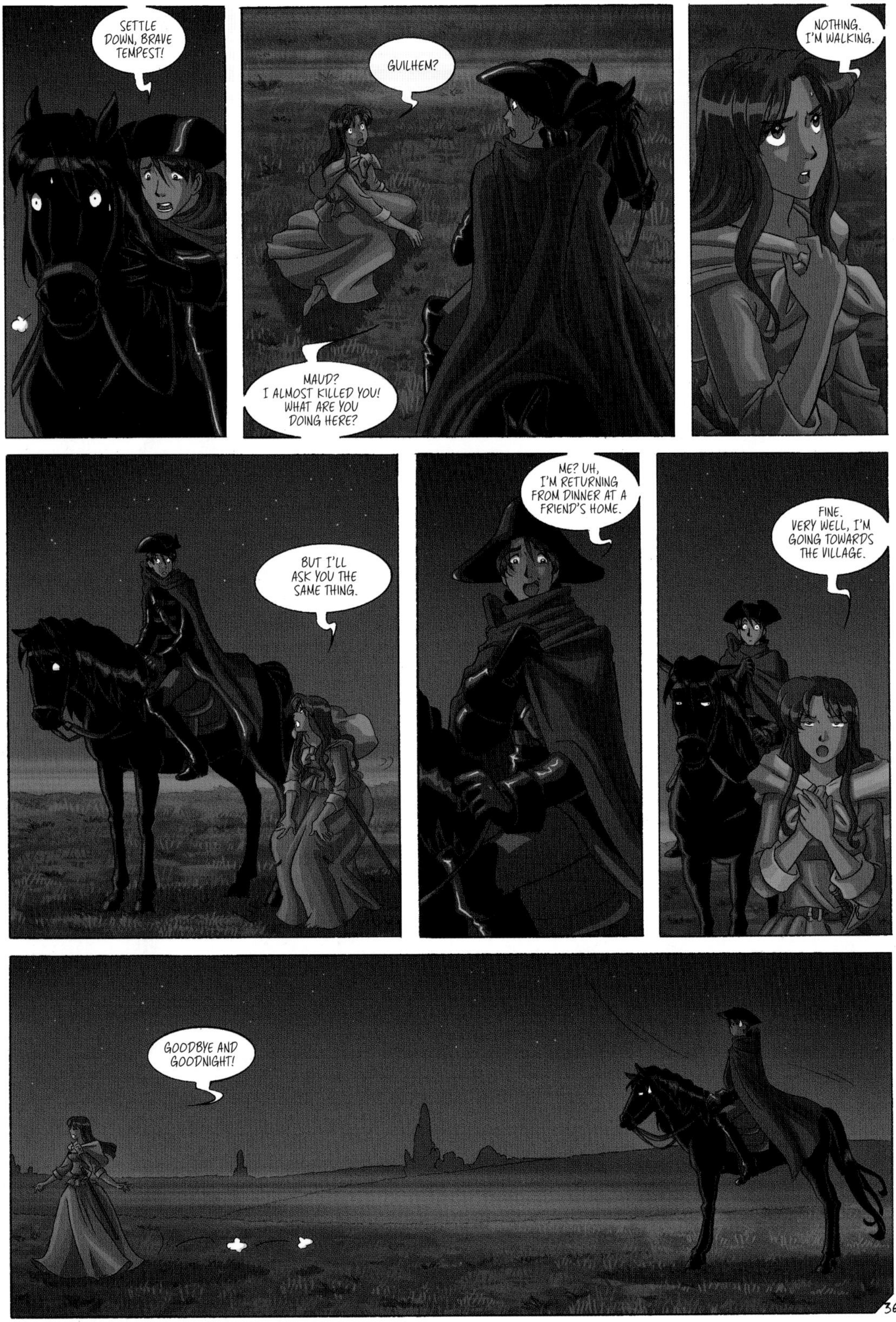
SETTLE DOWN, BRAVE TEMPEST!
GUILHEM?
MAUD? I ALMOST KILLED YOU! WHAT ARE YOU DOING HERE?
NOTHING. I'M WALKING.
BUT I'LL ASK YOU THE SAME THING.
ME? UH, I'M RETURNING FROM DINNER AT A FRIEND'S HOME.
FINE. VERY WELL, I'M GOING TOWARDS THE VILLAGE.
GOODBYE AND GOODNIGHT!
36

WAIT A SECOND!

YOU RAN AWAY FROM THE CONVENT?! I CAN'T LET YOU LEAVE. I'LL TAKE YOU BACK TO YOUR GRANDFATHER.

NO! I'D RATHER THROW MYSELF UNDER YOUR HORSE THAN GO BACK TO HIM!

I DON'T THINK TEMPEST WOULD APPRECIATE THAT. I CAN'T LEAVE YOU ALONE, IT'S TOO DANGEROUS!

COME WITH ME. MY HOME ISN'T FAR AWAY. WE'LL REVISIT YOUR SITUATION TOMORROW. WHAT'S MORE, SOMEONE WISHES TO SEE YOU AT THE CASTLE.

WHO'S THAT?

CLIMB ONTO MY HORSE AND YOU'LL SEE!

GIDDY UP, TEMPEST. TO CASTLE LANDREY!

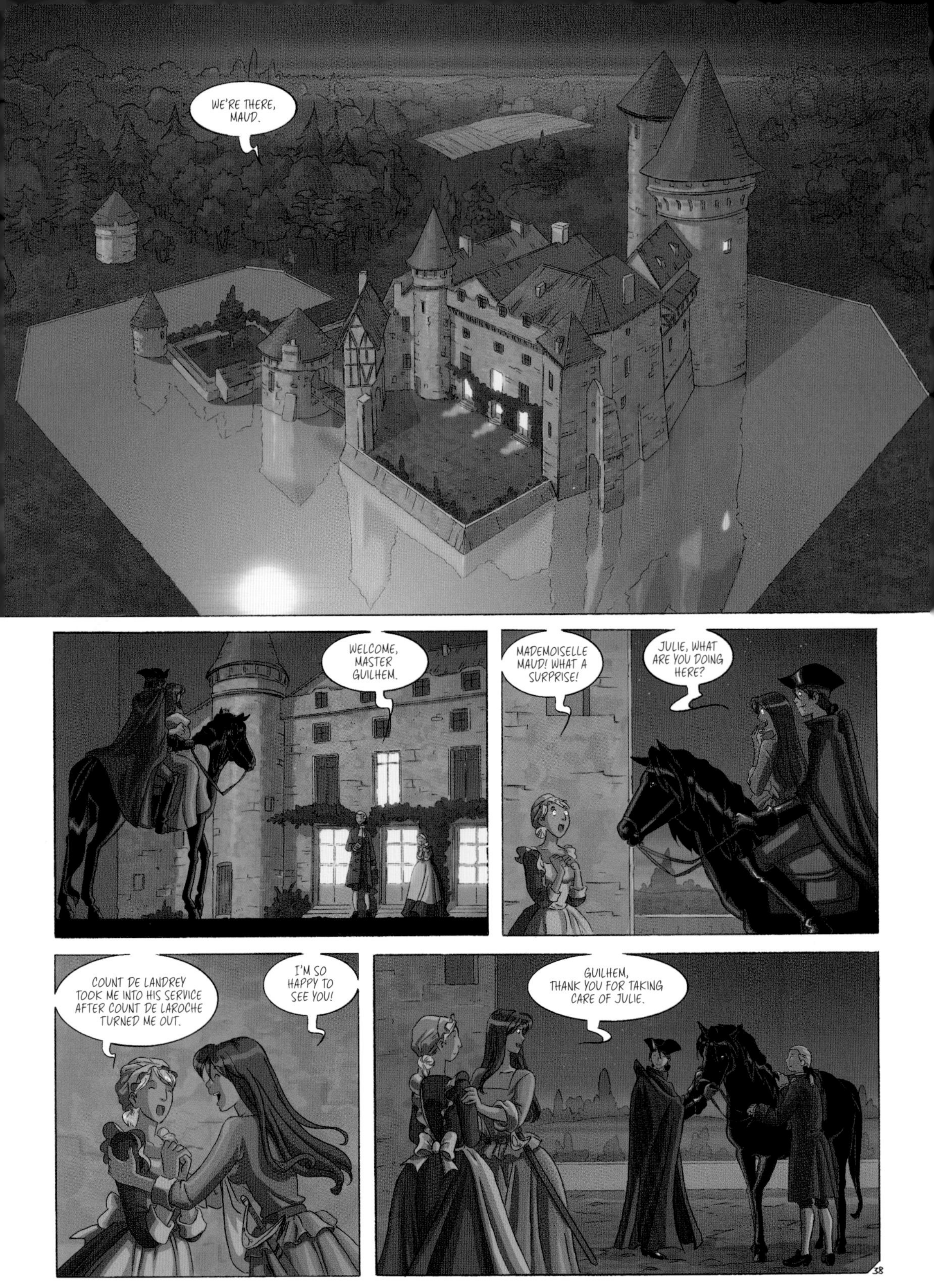
WE'RE THERE, MAUD.
WELCOME, MASTER GUILHEM.
MADEMOISELLE MAUD! WHAT A SURPRISE!
JULIE, WHAT ARE YOU DOING HERE?
COUNT DE LANDREY TOOK ME INTO HIS SERVICE AFTER COUNT DE LAROCHE TURNED ME OUT.
I'M SO HAPPY TO SEE YOU!
GUILHEM, THANK YOU FOR TAKING CARE OF JULIE.
38

IT'S MY FAULT, TOO, THAT JULIE WAS DISMISSED. AND ANYWAYS, SHE'S AN EXCELLENT EMPLOYEE!

THANK YOU, MR. GUILHEM. BUT YOU, MAUD, SHOULDN'T YOU BE AT THE CONVENT?

YES, BUT I RAN AWAY.

RAN AWAY? DOES COUNT DE LA ROCHE KNOW THAT YOU'RE HERE? HE MUST BE WORRIED!

I DON'T THINK SO. I'LL NEVER GO BACK TO HIM. TOMORROW I'M LEAVING FOR PARIS!

MEANWHILE, LET'S GO IN. WE ALL NEED A GOOD NIGHT'S SLEEP.

ALL THESE OBJECTS ARE YOURS?

THEY BELONGED TO MY PARENTS. THEY WERE GREAT TRAVELERS AND THEY BROUGHT THEM BACK FROM THEIR MANY TRIPS.

"WERE"?

THEY DISAPPEARED DURING A STORM AT SEA. THE SHIP CAPSIZED IN THE INDIAN OCEAN TWELVE YEARS AGO.

I MISS THEM, BUT I TELL MYSELF THAT, AT LEAST, THEY LIVED THEIR LIVES FULLY.

HERE'S YOUR ROOM, MAUD.

40

GUILHEM, PLEASE.

YES, MAUD?

DON'T SPEAK TO MY GRAND-FATHER OF MY ESCAPE. I DON'T WANT ANYTHING TO DO WITH HIM.

I'LL FIND WORK IN THE CITY AND CONTINUE TO SEARCH FOR MY FATHER'S KILLER.

THAT'S MADNESS, MAUD! I CAN'T LET YOU DO THAT! YOUR GRANDFATHER CARES ABOUT YOU. BELIEVE ME!

IF YOU SPEAK TO HIM, I'LL LEAVE IMMEDIATELY!

VERY WELL, I WON'T SAY ANYTHING.

I'VE MADE MY DECISION. I'LL DEPART TOMORROW. SINCE I'M HERE, I'LL TAKE MY FATHER'S NOTEBOOK BACK.

THE KILLER KNOWS YOU HAVE IT. I WOULDN'T WANT YOU TO BE IN EVEN MORE DANGER.

VERY WELL, I'LL RETURN IT TO YOU TOMORROW. I'VE HAD TIME TO STUDY IT A LITTLE. IT'S NOT AN EVERYDAY TRAVEL DIARY.

IN IT, YOUR FATHER DESCRIBES THE HABITS AND CUSTOMS OF THE OTTOMAN PEOPLE. DURING HIS TRIP, HE MEETS A PEOPLE PROTECTING A SACRED VALLEY THAT CONTAINS AN IMMENSE "POWER." EVEN STRANGER, THE FINAL PAGES HAVE BEEN TORN OUT. I SUPPOSE THAT'S DUE TO YOUR FATHER. THAT SECRET WASN'T TO BE DISCOVERED, AND I'M SURE THAT'S WHAT INTERESTS OUR KILLER!

A HIDDEN SECRET? BUT WHAT SORT OF POWER COULD BE HIDDEN THERE?

OBVIOUSLY, THERE'S NO PRECISE MAP.

THINKING ABOUT IT, BARON DE HUET ALLUDED TO THE TEMPLARS' SECRET. HE KNOWS MORE THAN HE SEEMS TO.

YOUR FATHER WRITES THAT THAT VALLEY WAS A STOPPING PLACE FOR THE TEMPLARS DURING THEIR CRUSADES.

YES, MAYBE THAT'S THE LINK!

ALL RIGHT, I PROPOSE YOU STAY HERE A FEW DAYS, GIVING US TIME TO FIND MORE INFORMATION ABOUT THAT PLACE. WE'LL SURELY FIND SOMETHING IN MY PARENTS' BOOKS.

FINE, LET'S LOOK TOGETHER, THEN I'LL LEAVE.

I'LL BE GOING. GOODNIGHT, MAUD.

?

SMAK

GOODNIGHT, GUILHEM, AND THANKS AGAIN FOR EVERYTHING YOU'RE DOING FOR ME.

TILL TOMORROW, THEN.

POOF

AH, THAT GUILHEM... IF THE FOX WEREN'T AROUND, I'D SURELY BE IN LOVE WITH HIM, HEE HEE HEE!

MADEMOISELLE MAUD, IT'S TERRIBLE!

HMM?

YOU MUST COME DOWN QUICK!

JULIE, WHAT'S GOING ON?

MAUD HAS RUN AWAY FROM THE CONVENT. I'M WORRIED. IF YOU HAVE ANY NEWS OF HER, LET ME KNOW.

YES, COUNT ON ME, MONSIEUR.

THANKS, GUILHEM.

GUILHEM!

!?

YOU HAVE BETRAYED ME AGAIN!

NO, ON THE CONTRARY.

MAUD?! WHAT ARE YOU DOING HERE?

OOPS!

COME, MAUD, YOUR GRANDFATHER IS WORRIED ABOUT YOU.

I DON'T WANT ANYTHING TO DO WITH HIM ANYMORE!

MAUD, WAIT!

I'M SORRY. I LIED TO YOU BECAUSE SHE THREATENED TO LEAVE.

I'M NOT ANGRY AT YOU, YOUNG GUILHEM.

KEEP HER HERE UNTIL SHE CALMS DOWN. YOU'RE MY FINAL HOPE FOR RECONCILING WITH HER.

44

CALM DOWN, MAUD. YOUR GRANDFATHER SIMPLY WANTED NEWS OF YOU.

SHUT UP! I DON'T BELIEVE YOU!

RETURN MY FATHER'S TRAVEL DIARY, AND LET'S BE DONE WITH EACH OTHER!

NO, YOU'RE GOING TO LISTEN TO ME! YOUR GRANDFATHER AGREED FOR YOU TO STAY HERE, TO REFLECT ON YOUR SITUATION.

I'M LEAVING IMMEDIATELY. I DON'T WANT TO SEE HIM OR YOU AGAIN!

I'M GOING TO FIND THE FOX! WE'LL AVENGE MY FATHER TOGETHER.

AND YOU'D DO EVERYTHING HE ASKS OF YOU?

OF COURSE, HE'S MY SOULMATE!

I'VE KNOWN THAT SINCE I FOUND OUT ABOUT HIM.

FINE, SINCE THAT'S HOW IT IS...

YOU MUST LISTEN TO ME, THEN.

TO BE CONTINUED...